molly o'malley
and the pirate queen

molly o'malley
and the pirate queen

by
Duane Porter

cover art
by
Karen Porter

Buried Treasure Publishing — Blue Springs

Molly O'Malley and the Pirate Queen

 This book is printed on acid-free paper.

Library of Congress Control Number 2010904821

Publisher's Cataloging-In-Publication Data

Porter, Duane.
  Molly O'Malley and the Pirate Queen / by Duane Porter ; cover art by Karen Porter. -- 1st ed.

  p. : ill. ; cm. -- (Molly O'Malley ; 3)

  Summary: Molly, a twelve-year-old girl from Chicago, is magically transported back in time to meet the Irish pirate queen Grace O'Malley.
  ISBN-13: 978-0-9800993-2-4
  ISBN-10: 0-9800993-2-3

  1. Leprechauns--Juvenile fiction. 2. Dragons--Juvenile fiction. 3. Ireland--Juvenile fiction. 4. Pirates--Juvenile fiction 5. Leprechauns--Fiction. 6. Dragons--Fiction. 7. Ireland--Fiction. 8. Pirates--Fiction. I. Porter, Karen. II. Title.

PZ7.P67 Mol 2010
[Fic]   2010904821

Published by **Buried Treasure Publishing**
Blue Springs MO 64015
www.buried**treasure**publishing.com

To David and Angie Porter
for all their support,
and to my nieces Madelyn and Jaden
for teaching me about ponies.

Acknowledgements

Some stories are so powerful that there must be a compelling truth behind them.

This book could not have been written without the extensive work of Anne Chambers, who became a primal force in resurrecting the memory of Grace O'Malley (Granuaile) for modern minds with her biography *Granuaile: Ireland's Pirate Queen; Grace O'Malley c.1530-1603*, first published in 1979. *Molly O'Malley and the Pirate Queen* relies heavily on Chambers' work to keep the story of Molly's adventures consistent within the known and accepted record of historical accounts. Believable fiction exists only within a trusted framework.

I also recommend Morgan Llywelyn's 1986 fictional work *Grania: She-King of the Irish Seas* for her excellent historical research. Our books share a closing scene with somewhat differing interpretations. Please note that Llywelyn's work is not intended for children!

A special thanks to my editors; Anita Mosley, Beth King, Linda Carrell; and to the Parkside Writers group and Cathy Porter for their editing and general comments on the story. Thanks also to the Northland critique group of the Midwest Children's Authors Guild.

My heartfelt thanks to Noel and Ita Walsh for their help with Gaelic pronunciation.

Of course, I owe the cover design once again to my talented daughter Karen. Thanks for sticking with your dad.

contents

how to say it
in irish

Name	Pronunciation
Achill	AH-kill (AH=a as in cat)
anamith	AH-nah-mih
bodhrán	BAW-rauwn
Bruionn	brinn
Bunowen	BUN-oh-wun
cathair	KAI-her
colleen	kai-LEEN
Connaught	kawn-AWKT
Connemara	kawn-ah-MAR-ah
currach	KUHR-awk
Croagh	kroak (*like a frog*)
Fannléas	fon-LAY-us
Finvarra	fin-VAR-ah
Fionn	fee-YON
Galway	GAWL-way
Grania	GRAWN-ya
Grainne Mhaol	grawn-yah-WAIL
Granuaile	grawn-yah-WAIL (English spelling)
Kildownet	kill-DOWN-et
la poupe (French)	la POOP
Labhras	LAW-ross

Name	Pronunciation
Lioc	LEE-ock
Lough Corrib	lok KOR-ib
Lough Mask	lok MAWSK
Mayo	MY-yo
Richard-an-Iarainn	Richard-awn-EYE-ah-rin
Roscommon	RAWS-kom-on
tanaiste	tah-NAWST-ah
Tiarnach	TEER-nauk

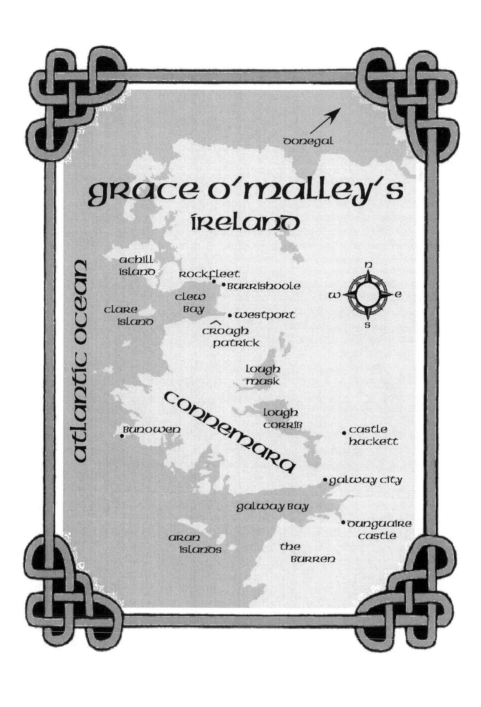

grace o'malley's
ireland

donegal

achill island

Rockfleet

• Burrishoole

clew Bay

clare island

• westport

croagh patrick

atlantic ocean

n
w e
s

lough mask

connemara

lough corrib

• castle hackett

Bunowen

• galway city

galway Bay

• ounguaire castle

aran islands

the Burren

chapter one

Visitors

O'Malley

*t*he ringfort appeared slowly in the distance above the cracked Burren hillside looking like a squat toad taking an afternoon nap. Molly looked anxiously at the ruins ahead before sneaking a quick glance behind her. "Are you doing all right, Aunt Shannon?"

Shannon chuckled. "I'm not as spry as I used to be, but I told ya I'd take ya up to the ringfort sometime! And here we are!"

Molly inhaled sharply as she glimpsed something red move quickly along the crest of the ringfort wall. *Be careful, Paddy,* she mouthed silently.

"Didja say something, Molly?"

"N-no, just catching my breath. We're almost there."

The pair approached the landmark wearily. "Let's jump the wall here, Molly. There's a wonderful view from the bay side I want to show ya." Shannon climbed over the low stone wall they had been following up the hillside and led the way toward the water.

"I'm glad to be back in Ireland," Molly said as she scrambled over the wall behind her aunt.

"Is that a fact now? Ya weren't any too happy when ya first arrived last summer, as I recall. What changed your mind?"

Maybe meeting a leprechaun, Molly thought. *But I can't tell you that part.* "Well, the Burren is pretty cool. It looks like a giant puzzle made out of flat rocks that have been spread out over the hills. Lots of flowers and ferns and everything grow in between them. You know how I like biology."

"This ringfort is built from the rocks of the Burren. The walls were built in a circle out of small stones all piled up. There are hundreds of ringforts like this one all over Ireland. No one knows who really built them." Shannon turned to whisper. "That's why another name for them is *fairy-fort.*"

They picked their way across the broken limestone to where the world seemed to open up around them. From their position high up on the hill facing the bay they could see a long distance in nearly every direction.

"We're just above the Black Head lighthouse." Shannon pointed. "There are the Aran Islands! Those mountains over there are part of Connemara. Of course, the water to the north here is Galway Bay. County Galway's just the other side — ya remember it from when we drove to Aillwee Cave along the coast road? And that's Galway City over on the northeast shore of the Bay."

"It's pretty," Molly agreed. "We only had a glimpse of this from the Mountain Walk at Aillwee Cave. But does anything exciting ever happen here? There are not many people that live here now, at least on the County Clare side."

"Oh, my, yes!" Shannon exclaimed. "They have boat races from Connemara to Kinvara each August. You've never seen a Galway hooker ship under full sail!"

"Not from the shore," Molly mumbled, remembering her voyage onboard the *Leela,* the thirty-foot Galway hooker ship that brought her from Chicago to Ireland in the world of Glimmer.

"Ya know, Grace O'Malley herself once sailed her fleet right through here into Galway City!" Shannon looked across the choppy waves longingly. "Now that would have been somethin' to see!"

"Who is Grace O'Malley?" Molly asked.

Her aunt turned and smiled at her. "She is probably the most famous relative ya have! Grace was a noble among the Gaelic chieftains in Ireland before the English took it over. She traded goods in Spain and Scotland, she was a pirate …"

"A *pirate?* A real pirate? But pirates are bad guys, aren't they?"

"Oh, Molly, it's a bit more complicated than that. Anyway, we're goin' to be finding out more about Grace when we take our trip north into County Mayo. That's where most of the O'Malley clan came from originally. Several of her castles are up there."

"So is she my great-great-great grandmother or something?" Molly asked.

"Not quite," Shannon laughed. "Grace O'Malley lived in the 16th century, over 400 years ago. And she wouldn't be a direct ancestor, even though we have the same O'Malley name, because the last name is generally passed on through men. But we're certainly kinfolk, and we should be proud of it."

"She sounds really cool. That was ages ago, though. The United States is only a little over 200 years old!"

"Ireland is an old country, dear. Many of the ruins left by people who lived here before are *very* old — the ringfort here is between eight hundred and sixteen hundred years old, no one's really sure. And some of the dolmens are six thousand years old!"

Shannon looked at her watch. "Speaking of time, your parents want to drive down to Doolin for dinner and stay for some music. And ya *know* how your Aunt Shannon loves traditional Irish music!" Shannon winked at her niece. "We should be gettin' back!"

Molly forced a smile. "Okay. Um — why don't you go on ahead? I want to peek inside the ringfort before going back. I've actually been up here before."

"I thought ya probably had. Ya spent a lot of time up here in the Burren last summer. I'll bet ya could lead tours yourself!" Shannon laughed. "Don't be too long!"

"I won't! I like the music too!" Molly breathed a sigh of relief. "I'll be right behind you!"

"Grand! Keep your eyes peeled for leprechauns. They're supposed to bring good luck!"

"If you say so, Aunt Shannon!" Molly called back, being careful not to let her voice squeak. *How does she do that? I know she doesn't believe in fairies, but it's spooky how what she says hits so close to the truth.*

She watched her aunt disappear down the hillside. Molly turned and walked around to the far side of the ringfort where the wall had crumbled, leaving an opening. As she stepped over the rocks, she could hear sharp metallic sounds echoing. Glancing up, she spotted a tiny man wearing a red shirt pounding rhythmically on a shoe with a miniature hammer.

Paddy tapped the final tack into the shoe and raised it to peer across the leather sole. "You've done yourself proud once again, Paddy me lad." He squinted as he glanced up toward the sun. "Now where is that girl?"

He looked down from his seat high on the ringfort wall and grinned.

Molly O'Malley smiled back at him, her arms folded in mock exasperation and a look of amused irritation wrinkling her freckled nose. "Paddy Finegan. I should have known. We just can't seem to avoid meeting here, can we?"

Paddy chuckled and planted his elbows on top of the wall, resting his chin in his tiny hands. "It's not as if ye haven't been stroking that enchanted bracelet all the way up the green road, now, is it me dear? I'd had to o' lost all o' me magic entirely to miss that ye were comin'. Besides, I think ye prefer this *cathair* to the dolmen."

"I do, if only because the ringfort is much closer to Aunt Shannon's. We *could* always meet at the pothole. Hardly anyone knows that it even exists besides us."

The leprechaun sighed. "I don't go there much any more. The cave feels lonely without the dragons. Don't get me wrong, I'm glad you used that last wish I granted ye to send both o' them back to Ellesyndria where they'd be safe. But Stanley was a rare companion, he understood things. And I know ye felt close to Nefra. At least they have each other now." Paddy stood up, stretching to his full two feet in height. "Would ye happen to have an extra apple with ye today, Molly?"

The red-haired girl picked her way over the jumbled ruins of the wall and found a seat on a large stone. She pulled a red-and-gold apple from her backpack and held it out. "It's a fuji apple. I kind of like them. They taste mostly sweet with just a little tart mixed in."

Paddy scampered down to get the apple. He took a big bite, nodding his approval. "Aye, that's a grand piece o' fruit. Now, me dear, we have a bit o' catchin' up to do."

"That's for sure." Molly rubbed her temples gently. "Paddy, I haven't seen you since we got back from Glimmer."

"*Fannléas,* the fairy world. I remember."

"It was an accident! I sent us there when I used the magic gold coin to rescue you."

"Aye, that was some rescue."

"Hush. Would you rather be goblin stew? Anyway, it's a place where ideas become *real.* At least, they were real inside Glimmer. But it wasn't just things inside the fairy world that changed. When I got home, the stories in a book of Irish fairy tales had changed, *too!* The people that we met in Glimmer were now characters in the stories. The book even talked about Corrigan and how she was responsible for most of the changelings."

"Interestin'. And did your storybook say who the leader o' the fairies is now?" Paddy dabbed at his chin with a tiny red handkerchief to catch some apple juice.

Molly smirked. "I would guess, my devious leprechaun friend, you've been doing some checking up on your own. My book says that a young prince named Fionn became the King of the Fairies. He's known as Finvarra now. And it's rumored that a human helped him at one time, which explains why he is kind to humans in return."

Paddy smiled. "I was just wantin' to check another source for accuracy. King Finvarra would be pleased to know that the humans writing down fairy tales got the story right."

Molly sat up straight. "You've talked to Fionn? How is he? Does he remember us?"

"No, I haven't talked to him. He keeps himself in Glimmer most o' the time, except when he comes to the human world to challenge someone to a game o' chess."

"Chess?"

"Aye, he loves the game. Never lost a challenge to a mortal, the stories say." Paddy took another bite from his apple. "And the stories are becomin' more reliable every day, it seems."

"Paddy, we changed history! Not just fairy history in Glimmer, but the books in the real world changed, too! Is that a bad thing?"

The leprechaun looked Molly sternly in the eye. "As I said when I sent ye home, I think it's a good thing. A wicked fairy was stopped, a vile creation was locked away once more, and a good and wise king now leads the fairies. Maybe we were lucky, but I'll take good luck anytime."

Molly sighed and let her shoulders sag. "It's so confusing. I guess I should stop worrying about it." Her face brightened. "The good news is that the cloth Queen Meb gave me is really cool! What do you think?" She stood with her arms outstretched to the side.

"I think if you spin around really fast with your hands tilted just right, ye might take off like a helicopter. What in blazes are ye talkin' about?"

"My sweater, silly. I made it out of the cloth." She touched the front with her palm and said quietly, *"Water."*

The green sweater shimmered slightly. "Now watch this," Molly said, and she ran a finger down the front from the neck to the waist. The material parted as smoothly as if she was sliding a zipper, *but there was no zipper.*

Paddy whistled. "That's a neat trick."

"It makes it really easy to get in and out of. I just have to be careful not to change it while other people are around. I have a feeling they wouldn't understand. Now check this out."

She slipped the sweater off of her arms and began stretching and pulling the material. First she shaped a large pocket, and then she pulled strings from the bottom corners to the opposite top corners, attaching them with a simple pinch. She looked at the result, nodded, and said *"Ice."*

The fabric stopped shimmering and took on the appearance of faded blue denim that matched her jeans. "It's one of my favorite forms, sort of a backpack purse. Anyway, it was starting to get too hot for the sweater."

"Very practical," Paddy grinned. "How long are ye here in Eire?"

Molly's face fell. "A couple of weeks. But only here at Aunt Shannon's until tomorrow. We're going to go up to County Mayo and rediscover our 'family roots.'"

"Ah, that's a shame. I was lookin' forward to spendin' more time with ye." Paddy finished the apple and looked at the core wistfully.

"Are you sure you weren't looking forward to the apple?" Molly grinned. "After Mayo, we're going on up to Donegal. I hope it's as beautiful as it was in Glimmer."

"Some things in Glimmer aren't so beautiful, Molly. Remember the *Anamith*."

Molly shivered. "The Soul Eater. Ooh, that thing still gives me the creeps just thinking about it. Not to mention that horrible Corrigan."

"I'm sure you'll find Donegal to your liking. Just you and your mom and dad going?"

"No!" Molly's face brightened. "Aunt Shannon is coming with us! It'll be great!"

"Oh, that'll be grand, Molly! I know how close ye are to your aunt. Say, going back to Glimmer for a moment ..."

"Yes?"

"Ye know how none o' the magic we had from the real world worked while we were in Glimmer?"

"Uh-huh, but I thought we figured out that was because they were designed to pull their magic power from Glimmer into the real world."

"Aye. I think that was right for the bracelet and the coin. Me own magic spells worked the same way until I adapted to bein' there. But I've been thinkin' about your medallion."

Molly's hand closed on the stone circle under her shirt. "Why would this be any — oh. I see what you're saying. When we were testing the medallion's power to translate between Irish and English, it worked just fine while we were still in Glimmer. What does that mean, Paddy?"

"Either the medallion has a very special enchantment designed to work from either Glimmer or the real world, or it isn't a fairy enchantment at all. It may have magic that's beyond the fairy world altogether."

Molly stared at the leprechaun with her mouth hanging open. "There's magic outside the fairy world?"

Paddy flicked the apple core to a seagull that had descended to the ringfort wall. "It wasn't too long ago ye would o' said the real world was the *only* thing that existed."

"Not any more," Molly sighed. "I suppose there's always something new to learn about. I thought school was out for the summer."

"Ah, life is a school, Molly dear," Paddy smiled. "Trust this old leprechaun on that."

She pulled the medallion out and looked closely at it. "This is the only thing I have left of Nefra."

"You've got that long skinny black band that I saved for ye."

"Oh, that thing. It held the medallion around Nefra's neck for centuries until I took it off. It's all worn and black and disgusting. I don't even know why I kept it. This gold chain that your friend Kevin gave me works much better to hang the medallion on."

"Aye, the gold's just the right length for your neck."

"Well, I'd better get going. I don't want to make Aunt Shannon and my folks late for dinner and music." She gave Paddy a tight hug. "I'll come back if I can. Take care of yourself."

"I will, Molly. You be careful, too."

"No problem. Aunt Shannon says leprechauns are supposed to bring good luck!" She grinned and skipped away over the flat-topped rocks.

Paddy climbed back to his perch high atop the ringfort wall to watch the red-haired girl disappear down the Burren hillside. "I can't say I ever brought ye good luck, Molly dear," he whispered. "But ye always seem to be able to do good in every place ye find yourself!"

chapter two

Rockfleet

The O'Malleys traveled north after driving along the coast road to Kinvara. Molly pressed her face to the window as they passed Dunguaire Castle at a wide, sweeping turn in the road. "I still can't get over how close the castles are to the roads in Ireland," she murmured.

Aunt Shannon smiled at Molly across the back seat they shared as she replied. "Remember that when these castles were built, they were the center of everything. They built the roads to make it easy to get there. During times of war, everyone needed to be able to get into the castle quickly, including the local residents. Most of the modern roads are just paved over where the old roads had been before."

The weather forecast predicted hot and sunny conditions, so Molly had pulled on a pair of black capris and a light yellow buttoned shirt. Since the day promised more driving and touring than hiking, she wore simple black flats instead of her boots. She held her special backpack purse in her lap.

Several hours later they arrived at the town of Westport. "Look!" Molly cried. "There's a mountain over there!"

"That's not just any mountain, Molly. That's Croagh Patrick, the holy mountain of St. Patrick himself," Aunt Shannon said. "In ancient times it was supposed to be the home of the Celtic gods, kind of like their local Mount Olympus. Patrick knew that as a Christian missionary he would have to challenge the pagan beliefs before he could preach the gospel of Christ. So he climbed the mountain and fasted there forty days. When he returned, the people said that he must have conquered the old gods to have survived, and they listened to his preaching. Now tens of thousands of pilgrims follow the tradition of climbing the mountain to worship and celebrate St. Patrick's victory. It's said that Patrick built the church that is at the top. Ya might be able to see the church from here."

"Yeah, I think I see something up there. That's pretty cool, with the mountain sitting so close to the water."

"The water is Clew Bay," Molly's father said. "We're getting right into the old stomping grounds of Grace O'Malley herself. She had castles built all around the bay. Do you see the island out there? That's Clare Island. It's got a pretty good-sized mountain itself."

"Why, Sean," Shannon remarked with a grin. "You've been studying your Irish history! I thought ya didn't care for all that 'Irish roots' nonsense."

"Well, big sister, I figured I needed to get up to speed. I have a daughter who has talked about nothing but Ireland since she came to visit you last summer!" He smiled in the rear-view mirror. "And since I'm driving, I needed to know where we were going anyway!"

"Wait a minute," Molly said. "Are you talking about Grace O'Malley, the pirate Aunt Shannon told me about?"

"That's right," Sean O'Malley nodded. "We're in County Mayo now, and this is the heart of O'Malley territory."

They turned down a winding road that led through a park-like estate. A huge grey mansion came into view, nestled beside a river that flowed into a blue lake. Stately trees stood along the shore, with Clew Bay still visible beyond. Croagh Patrick towered above the scenery from only a few miles away.

Molly looked at the sign that read 'Westport House.' "Is this where Grace O'Malley lived?"

"I'm not clear on that," Shannon said. "Westport House wasn't built until the 1700s, which was after Grace's time, but I seem to remember a connection of some kind. Let's ask the guides inside."

Westport House had a large parking lot and a steady flow of visitors. Molly's dad paid the admission fees and they joined the next tour. "You didn't want to go to the Pirate Adventure Park too, did you sport?" he asked Molly.

Molly shook her head. "From that poster, it looks like an Irish amusement park. I can ride the Logger's Run at Six Flags Great America if I want a flume ride. I want to find out more about the *real* pirate."

Kate O'Malley gave her daughter a hug. "You're turning out to be quite the historian, dear! What happened to the biology and science you were interested in last year?"

"Oh, I'm still interested in those. I just think history is really important, too."

"Important?" Molly's dad raised an eyebrow. "A twelve-year-old likes something important over something fun?"

Molly turned to look at her dad, lanky and relaxed, rubbing her mom's shoulders. She took a deep breath. "Yeah, Dad," she said. "Sometimes you have to take care of the important things before you can have fun."

"Out of the mouths of babes," Shannon whispered and looked at her brother Sean intently.

He nodded and stepped over to Molly, embracing her tightly. "You're absolutely right, honey. I had to take care of the important things, like spending more time with your mother and you instead of my job. Until I did that, our family life wasn't much fun, was it?"

Molly squeezed back. "Thanks for understanding, Dad. I love you."

Stepping into the entrance hall, they saw a number of arched doorways that rose to a coffered ceiling made of squares that were sunken to give a 3-D effect. The center of the ceiling rose in a magnificent barrel arch. To the side twin braces of crossed swords hung on white painted wood columns flanking a sweeping marble staircase. On the first landing a carved statue of an angel stood alone in a scarlet alcove. The staircase split at the angel's feet, rising and twisting yet again to reach the next floor.

"Wow," Molly murmured. "Talk about making an entrance."

Their guide, a young woman in her twenties overheard. "Westport House was designed by the noted architects Richard Cassels and James Wyatt. Mr. Cassels conceived the barrel ceiling you see here. James Wyatt was a famous painter, too, and we have some of his works on display."

Each room was finished in great detail. Molly especially liked the spacious dining room, decorated with unusual pictures made right into the walls and ceiling. The thin wooden oval frames glowed with a pleasing yellow hue. Backgrounds of light, cheerful solid blue surrounded classic white figures raised in bas relief. "Those look familiar somehow," she whispered to her mother.

"They look like Wedgwood Jasperware, only they're not pottery," her mother replied. "I think they make the pottery in England. It's the same type of design, right down to the matte finish. Whoever designed this room sure liked the look of it, didn't they?"

"What's matte?"

"That's when you don't make it shiny. Most pottery has a glaze to protect it, and it becomes shiny when it's fired in the kiln. But Wedgwood's Jasperware is not glazed, so the finish stays dull."

During the tour they found that Westport House was still owned by the direct descendents of Grace O'Malley. "Did Grace O'Malley ever live here?" Molly asked their guide.

"In a sense," the guide replied. "Westport House is built on the foundations of the old O'Malley castle. We'll see that as part o' the tour; we call it the dungeon now. Grace lived in the castle from time to time, but her favorite castle was Rockfleet."

"Is Rockfleet near here?"

"About twenty kilometers from here on the northeast corner of Clew Bay. It's been restored, so it's still in fairly good shape."

"Dad, can we see Rockfleet?" Molly begged.

"I don't see any reason why not. It's probably the last thing we'll be able to see today, though. It's been a long day for this Irishman."

"Sean, it's so *grand* to hear y'talk like that!" Shannon grasped his arm and leaned her head against his shoulder. "Ya really *are* comin' back to your Irish roots!"

"It's been a long time," he murmured. "But it feels good." He grinned at Molly and winked. "It feels good to be Irish."

———

Rockfleet was a vast change from the lavish and ornate Westport House. They found the castle standing on the lonely coastline, a simple four-sided stone tower that rose fifty feet from where the water lapped at its base.

A few stone steps led into the lower level, which had a simple dirt floor. Surprisingly, there were no steps to the second level, only a wooden ladder.

"They must have used the ladder so they could pull it up behind them during a siege," Shannon mused. "Be careful climbing up — every other step on the ladder is different. It's like a spiral staircase, where one side is wider than the other, but it switches back and forth on this thing."

They found the second floor had a corridor that ran around the outside walls, presumably for defense. The floor was made of wood here. An inner chamber was lit only by the narrow slit windows from the corridor. A narrow stone spiral staircase led up to the next level.

As they climbed to the third level Molly asked, "Do they have a fireplace on each floor?"

"They sure do, honey," her father responded. "That's the only way they could heat it back then."

The third level was spacious, with an arched ceiling made of stone, and another wooden floor. A great fireplace stretched across one wall. "Looks like the great hall," said Shannon. "Can you imagine the feasts they had in here?"

"How many more floors are there?" Molly groaned.

"Just one more, right, Sean?" Kate asked her husband.

"I think so, dear. That should be Grace O'Malley's private quarters."

As they climbed the next set of stone spiral steps, they were surprised to find that Grace O'Malley's bedroom was not the next thing they came to. A small stone room came first, with a window open to the outside. A crude seat was fashioned in the stone with a hole in it. "Ah, the privy," Aunt Shannon nodded. "Also sometimes called a garderobe."

"You mean it's a bathroom? Why would they have an open window in a bathroom?" Molly wondered.

"Think about it, Molly," Shannon giggled. "It would smell pretty bad if there wasn't a way to get lots of fresh air in here. I imagine there is a pipe that runs through the wall down to the water. The high tide would wash all of the waste away."

Molly paused to look at Croagh Patrick framed in the little bathroom window. "At least they had a nice view."

A few more steps and they reached the top floor. The great hall below with its stone ceiling allowed this room to have a floor made of flagstones instead of wood. The fireplace sat cold and dark along the wall. Another set of stone steps led up, apparently to the rooftop from the amount of light showing, but an iron gate barred the entrance. Timbers angled up from the walls to meet in the middle, forming a high ceiling.

"I guess this is as far as we go," Sean said, rattling the gate lightly.

"We're standing where Grace O'Malley slept!" Shannon's eyes were glowing. "Isn't this exciting, Molly?"

"I guess so. I just expected something … nicer, I suppose. I know there's no furniture in here or anything, but it's hard to imagine anyone really *living* here."

Kate O'Malley ruffled her daughter's hair lovingly. "Not everything was nice back then. But from what little I've heard of Grace O'Malley, she would have had *something* nice in here."

At that moment Molly felt a chill run down her spine. She stared across the room, not believing what she saw.

"Well, nothing else to see here. Let's head back to the car and find our Bed & Breakfast." Molly's dad paused when he reached the spiral stairs. "Watch your footing on these steps, now, Kate. Everyone take it easy going down."

"Right behind you," Molly whispered, not really caring if he heard her or not.

As Aunt Shannon disappeared down the stairway, Molly walked over to the wall to look more closely at her startling find.

Engraved into the stone was a strange pattern. It was a circle, and the center looked like an eye, with a pupil like a cat's, thin and vertical. Around that was a grooved circle with a larger indented spot. When she looked at the strange spot closer, it appeared to be a snake's head devouring the rest of its own body. A large triangle surrounded the eye and the snake.

"I know this!" she said softly.

Trembling, she pulled the heavy stone necklace from beneath her shirt. The medallion hung from a golden chain around her neck. She looked at the medallion's face with its engravings, then at the wall again.

The engravings were identical, except the one on the wall was reversed, like looking in a mirror.

"How is this possible?" she gasped. Molly held her medallion closer to the engraving on the wall to better compare them. As she did, she touched the wall with her medallion.

The carving on the wall vanished in a bluish glow.

"What? Where did it go?" She touched the place where it had been with her fingers, then paused and looked slowly around.

Where the wall just to her left had been bare moments before, a thick sheepskin now hung over it. A fire crackled merrily in the fireplace, and a bed sat in the corner, covered with pillowed blankets made of rich silk. The stairs leading up to the castle ramparts were no longer barred, but open to the stars.

A creak sounded behind her, and Molly whirled in a panic to see what it was.

The door from the stairway leading up from the great hall opened wide, thudding into the wall tapestry. A tall woman stepped into the room, wearing short trousers and a bloused shirt, topped with a short leather vest. Her face looked worn and weather-beaten in the firelight, and her jet-black hair was peppered with flecks of grey. She looked haggard and tired, as though she were carrying a great weight.

Then she noticed Molly and her demeanor changed in an instant.

Her hand moved like lightning to her belt and a knife appeared, flashing in the yellow firelight. She crouched as a wrestler might, her weight balanced perfectly on the balls of her feet.

Molly dared not breathe, dared not move, dared not cry out, staring in shock at the woman who was poised like a tiger ready to spring.

The woman straightened slightly, blinked as if adjusting to the light, and said, "What are ya doing in me room, child?"

chapter three

Adrift

olly's head swam. She stretched her hand to the rough stone wall to steady herself. "What am I doing in ..." She looked at the tall stranger as feelings of confusion and despair washed over her. "I — I don't know." She met the tall woman's gaze, seeing the fire's reflection glistening in those dark eyes. "*Your* room? Who — who are you?"

The woman threw back her head and laughed, a deep throaty explosion. "I haven't been away *that* long now, have I?" She chuckled and slid the knife easily back into its sheath. "Whose room do ya *think* it is, child? Surely ya know whose castle it is you're in!"

Molly felt the blood drain from her face. "No, it can't be ... that's impossible. It *can't* be ..." She looked at the warrior-woman before her, and then to the crackling fireplace. "Oh, who am I kidding? It happened *again?* Oh no, oh no, no ..." The girl stumbled to the bed and threw herself down on the silk pillows, pounding them in frustration.

She felt a gentle hand touch her back. "There, there child, it's all right. Tell me your name, now. We'll start with that."

Molly turned angry eyes to the strong woman now seated beside her. "It's *not* all right. You don't understand! I'm not supposed to be here!"

"Your *name*, child." The woman's voice radiated authority.

"M-Molly. Molly O'Malley."

"Well, you're kin, then, and under my protection. There's nothin' to fear. Interestin' cloth in your blouse, child. Did that come from Spain?"

"Kin?" Molly ignored the comment about her shirt as a memory of Aunt Shannon flooded back to her. If what she feared was true … "Mrs. O'Malley. May I ask you a question?"

"First of all, it's *Granuaile*. O'Malley is me family name, not me married name. That would be Bourke now, had I not dismissed Iron Richard from the walls of this very castle. Rockfleet has been mine for these thirteen years."

"Grawnya-wail?" Molly sounded the name out. "Your name is bald Grace?"

"Or just *Grania* for short. Granuaile is a family nickname. When I was nine my father told me I could not sail with him. He said my hair would get in the way and girls had no business on board a ship anyway. I cut my own hair off, dressed in boy's clothes and sneaked aboard." Grania's eyes twinkled. "He was angry for a bit, but he didn't throw me off the ship. The family started calling me Granuaile — Grania the Bald — and the name stuck."

"All right. Grania, then. What year is it?"

The woman slowly leaned back, surprised. "That's a mighty strange question. Well, just so ya don't lose track of it again, this is the year of our Lord 1579."

Molly nodded woodenly. "I expected an answer close to that."

"Where are your parents then, Molly?"

Molly continued to stare straight ahead. "I have no parents in this world."

Grania watched her expression closely. "I believe ya, child." She sighed deeply and put her arms around Molly's shoulders. "Now *you* believe *me*. You're an O'Malley, and you're part o' my family now, if ya wish. Will ya accept my protection, Molly?"

Molly turned and was struck how worn and exhausted Grania looked. Closer to the fireplace she could see that her eyes were blue, or possibly even green like her own. "You'd do that for me? Of course I'll accept. I'm grateful for your help." She hugged the older woman tightly, and was somewhat surprised to feel Grania squeeze back.

"Grania — are ... are you all right?"

Grania O'Malley stiffened for an instant as if she had suddenly gone somewhere else. Then she looked at Molly with wonder in her eyes.

"I've been rotting in prison for the past two years, the last four months in the English dungeon o' Dublin Castle. I only returned to Rockfleet yesterday. I've had hardship in me life before, but captivity ..." she shuddered and squeezed Molly again. "I practically grew up on the deck of a ship, sailing under God's great sky. To be locked away from the sun and the wind for all this time — I don't know how I survived."

"I'm sorry," Molly whispered. "I didn't know. I was just a little surprised when you hugged me just now. You're a pirate, right? I didn't think pirates did things like that."

Grania laughed again, hugging Molly all the tighter. "Aye, I'm a pirate! I'm a mother, too, with four children of me own! I lead the clan O'Malley, several hundred o' the clan O'Flaherty and I take care of all o' them. But most of all I'm alive! I'll face the devil himself if I must to survive and protect me family and friends!" She looked fondly at the red-haired girl in her arms. "And you'll survive too, Molly O'Malley! You've got the fire in you the same as me, that's for sure! *'You're a pirate, right?'* Ha, that's grand!"

"You're not mad at me?" Molly's eyes were like saucers.

"Not a bit. I imagine I like ya because you're wearing trews like me instead of a dress. Not a common thing for an Irish girl to do! Oh, well ..." Grania rubbed her temple gingerly. "I wonder if I'm gettin' a headache. Half the time when ya say something, me head gets the slightest buzz, like an echo."

"Oh." Molly carefully tucked the stone medallion back inside her shirt. *She must be hearing my voice inside her head, the way I did when Nefra was wearing the medallion.* "Maybe I should leave. In fact, could one of your ships take me to Donegal?"

"Donegal? Why would ya want to go to Donegal?"

To find the Fairy King Finvarra at Castle Tiarnach. He might be able to help me get home. "I've been enough trouble to you, Grania. I-I've been thinking about going to Donegal anyway, and ..."

"I've had too many sea captains try to lie to me about the cargo their ship carried. Don't think I'm fooled with this fairy tale o' *yours,* Molly O'Malley!" Grania's eyes flashed midnight-blue, but her lips betrayed a trace of amusement.

"Granuaile?" The slim woman wearing a simple shift paused at the door, standing as silently as she had entered. Her eyes crinkled at the corners, hinting at a zest for life that belied her obvious age. "Who do we have here?"

"El, just the person I wanted to see! This is Molly o' the clan O'Malley. She'll be stayin' with us now, the girl has no parents. Molly, Elva is me housekeeper and is worth more than ten sailors. She'll find a bed for ya tonight." Grania stood up, lifting Molly firmly by her elbow.

Elva smiled warmly as she reached to take Molly's hand. "I'll put her in my own cottage for the night. My children are grown, and Liam won't be home from fishing until tomorrow. A bed will be better than a mat on the ground."

"Thank you — thank you both!" Molly accepted Elva's hand nervously and started with her toward the door.

"Molly, one more thing," Grania called after her. "How old are ya?"

Molly turned back, surprised. "Twelve. Why?"

Grania nodded with satisfaction. "You'll find out tomorrow. Elva, are ya thinkin' what I'm thinkin'?"

Elva grinned and her eyes danced. "I wouldn't presume to boast that I think like the Queen o' Connaught. But yes, I think they would be good for each other. Give them something to do, keep them out o' trouble."

"Good, because I'm going to keep ya very busy for the next few days. We've a castle to put back in order, and I need to inspect the boats." Grania stretched and Molly thought she could have been watching a sleek panther preparing to bed down for the night. "We'll talk more in the morning, Molly. Rest well."

Elva led Molly down the spiral staircase. The privy reeked a little as they passed by, betraying its recent use. "Need to use it before we leave the keep, young lady?" Elva asked.

Molly shook her head. "We're leaving the castle?"

"Most everyone lives outside the castle. There's not much room and the place would be stinking in no time with everyone crammed in here."

They entered the grand hall to find a woman poking the remnants of a blaze in the great fireplace. A long wooden table flanked by benches stretched beneath the arched stone ceiling, and several giant turtle shells varnished to a bright sheen adorned the walls.

"Elva," Molly said as they descended the stairs to the second level, "what did you mean when you said that 'they' would be good for each other?"

"Just what I said, mistress. 'They' are made up of you and another person, who will arrive on the morrow. The thought seemed to amuse Granuaile, and since she didn't offer up any names, I'll not be the one to spoil her fun." Elva reached the bottom of the stairwell and stepped into the corridor. She turned, wearing a huge smile, and whispered, "Don't worry. I think it'll be fun for you, too!"

"Just what I need. Another mystery." Molly sighed but smiled back as best she could. She peeked through one of the vertical slit windows. "Is that a ship?"

Elva stooped to look. "Aye, that's Granuaile's galley. The others have gone to — well, let's just say they'll be back within the week."

"Galley? Isn't that like a kitchen?"

The woman eyed Molly curiously. "Ye haven't spent much time near the sea, have ye?" Molly shook her head. "A galley is a ship that can be rowed with oars. The ships in Granuaile's fleet have sails as well. The oars are used mainly when there is little or no wind, or when speed or precise navigation is needed."

"Oh, that makes sense. Thank you for being patient with me."

"Well, ye are very polite for one with so many questions. Watch your step on the ladder, now." Elva climbed carefully down a ladder quite similar to the one Molly had used to climb up, but this ladder looked old and worn in comparison.

Stacks of great axes, blue-grey gun muzzles and bright spearheads set in wooden shafts glittered from their piles leaning against the walls in the lowest level. Swords and daggers hung above them, secure in their leather scabbards. Several lanterns lit the room, their flickering flames dancing as they bounced off the considerable armaments everywhere.

They passed through the door to the outside, stepping between two men holding muskets. They nodded to Elva as she went out. "Goodnight," she called cheerily, and led Molly toward a group of buildings.

Molly shivered from the sudden chill. "Brrr. Um — what month is it?"

"It's the seventh day o' March. By Brigid, ye have a lot o' questions! And before ye ask, *that's* a galley," Elva pointed to the ship floating in the nearby bay under the half-moon, "and *that's* the kitchen." She turned to present a long, low building a good stone's throw from the castle walls.

"Wouldn't it be easier to have the kitchen inside the castle?" Molly asked.

"What am I going to do with ye, girl? We keep the kitchen out here *away* from the castle. Do ye want to burn the castle down? Besides, it would get too hot during the summer when you're cooking."

"I'm sorry. I have a lot to learn."

Elva paused with her hands on her hips. "It's all right, child. I just don't have much time to teach ye everything properly. This place has been so busy with Granuaile finally coming back ..." She pushed her hair back and sighed. "But she's here now, and things are going to get back to normal. As normal as things can be anyway, with the greedy English moving in."

They continued past the kitchen to a prim wooden cottage with a thatched roof. "Here's home for the night, Molly. Let's get ye inside."

A single room held a double bed near a fireplace that needed stoking badly. Several chairs ringed a general living area, and a ladder made of poles led up to a loft.

"There's a bed in the loft for ye. It'll give ye a bit o' privacy up there." Elva picked up a stick and jammed it into the embers, waking them to life before throwing another brick of peat onto the fire.

"Thank you. I appreciate all that you're doing for me."

"Oh, don't mention it. Now up to bed with ye. Here's a nightgown to wear. I still have a few things to take care of."

Molly climbed the ladder and inspected her room. The ceiling hung close above her bed, and a small shuttered window looked out toward the bay. The bed itself had a mattress with a low mahogany frame. "Better than sleeping on just straw, that's for sure," she whispered under her breath.

She heard the cottage door close as Elva left. Molly changed into the nightgown and snuggled under the thin green blanket. "Okay," she sighed, "the best I can figure is that the medallion somehow transported me here, just like the golden coin that Paddy gave me did before. I was thinking of Grace O'Malley — *Grania* — *Granuaile* — I was in her *bedroom*, for goodness sake — and that must have pulled me here. I *must* be in Glimmer. That's the only explanation that makes any sense."

She lay still, listening to the night sounds of the few people still moving around outside and the water of Clew Bay lapping gently on the shore. "Only this time I'm by myself, and I have no idea how to get back to the real world. What are my chances of finding Fionn or Castle Tiarnach on my own? What are my chances of ever seeing my family again? Grania already suspects — no, she *knows* that I'm not telling the whole truth." She gripped the stone disk tightly. "I don't know if this medallion is the key, or if it was a one-way ticket like the coin was. I need ... I need to ... keep my eyes open ..."

Then, alone in her loft on the grounds of Rockfleet castle, in the year of our Lord 1579, Molly O'Malley closed her eyes and quietly cried herself to sleep.

chapter four

Toby

*t*he thumping of Elva's broom handle on the floorboards woke her before the sound of the rooster's crowing registered. "Get up, miss, or there'll be no breakfast for ye!"

Molly groaned and rubbed the sleep from her eyes. "Coming," she yawned, and began pulling on her clothes. She slid her trusty folding hairbrush from her pocket and smoothed most of the tangles from her hair before clambering down from the loft.

Elva stirred the contents of a sooty cast-iron pot suspended on a great hook over the fireplace. "The porridge is fresh, at any rate. Our food isn't as good as it was a few years back, but Granuaile hasn't been trading for a while. Wash up first, the pitcher is against the wall. Then get some of this down ye or you'll be late." She ladled a great, oozing dollop of porridge into a bowl and set it on the table.

Molly poured a few inches of water from the porcelain pitcher into the matching bowl and splashed the cool liquid on her face and arms. "Late for what?" she sputtered as she groped for a towel.

"Ye'll not know if ye don't hurry, now, will you?" Elva snorted good-naturedly as she thrust the towel into Molly's outstretched hand. "There's a pitcher o' milk on the table."

"Any brown bread?"

"Do you think you're in Dublin, now? The men have done well to catch fish and do a bit o' trading, but things have been a bit difficult with Granuaile gone." Elva grinned as she unwrapped a steaming hot loaf of brown bread. "Lucky for ye we laid in a good store o' flour before she was captured during the raid on Desmond."

"Mmmm, that smells delicious! The raid on what?"

"The Earl o' Desmond. That's what started the trouble two years ago, when Granuaile raided his homeland. Desmond imprisoned her at Limerick for a year and a half, then turned her over to the English to save his own neck. She's lucky to be back here in one piece. Now eat, girl!"

Molly dutifully bolted down her breakfast and then followed Elva out of the cottage. Grania was already outside the castle talking with two horsemen who had apparently just come down the road. One of the riders was a boy about her age, the other a gentleman old enough to be his father. Grania embraced the boy as he dismounted, and put her mouth close to his ear as Elva and Molly approached.

"Good morning, Granuaile!" Elva called out. Grania stood and faced them with her arm draped over the boy's shoulders.

"Good morning, Elva, Molly! Didja sleep well, dear?"

Molly shrugged in reply. "After a while. Strange place and everything."

Grania's bright blue eyes danced in the sunlight. "I thought you'd like someone ta show ya around today. This is me son, Tibbot-ne-Long Bourke."

The boy nodded in greeting, his crystal blue eyes gorgeous under a full head of curly blond hair. His smile parted into a grin as he said, "I'm glad to meet you!"

Molly smiled back. "Did your mom just say your name is Toby-of-the-Ships?"

Toby's eyes registered surprise for a moment, then he smiled and looked up at his mother who nodded back. "That's right! Quite a mouthful, isn't it? You can just call me Toby."

"Thank you, Toby! I'll want to hear how you got that name if you have time later. Is this your dad?"

"This is my foster father, Edmund MacTibbot. My real father is Richard-in-Iron."

"The same Richard that your mom locked out of Rockfleet Castle?" Molly asked, looking between Toby and Grania.

"Yes, the very same," Toby grinned. "But now I live with my foster family near my real father's holdings in Burrishoole. We rode down this morning after we found that Mam would be here."

"Is Burrishoole far?" Molly asked.

"About three miles. Hardly enough for the ponies to break a sweat." Toby patted the massive shoulder of his steed.

Molly smiled. "Your pony is beautiful. Do you ride much?"

"Just about every day, in between sword fighting lessons, axe fighting, archery ..."

"You spend every day learning how to fight?"

"You didn't let me finish. I read books, have my Latin lessons, study accounting ..."

Molly shook her head. "You're way too busy to have to show me around. I don't want to be a bother."

"You're not a bother," Toby said firmly. "I'm taking the day off from my studies and I can use the diversion. Let's see ... do you like stories?"

Molly's eyes lit up. "I *love* stories!"

"Well then, Mam, could you tell her about Castlekirk?"

"Oh, that was a few years back!" Grania laughed. "One story, then. My first husband was Dónal O'Flaherty, but he was known as Dónal o' the Battles because he loved to fight. The Joyces were a rival clan and Dónal captured their island castle."

"I guess the Joyces didn't like that," Molly mused.

"Not a bit. They started calling it Cock's Castle, for when they tried to recapture Castlekirk, Dónal defended it so fiercely that the Joyces gave him a new nickname — Dónal the Cock. It suited Dónal perfectly," Grania chuckled. "He was always one to strut about like a rooster. That was his weakness. He always pushed things too far. When Dónal went off on another one o' his raids, the Joyces ambushed and killed him. They thought it would be easy to recapture the castle after that."

"They reckoned wrong, though," Edmund laughed. "They reckoned without considering Granuaile."

"All this nonsense about women staying at home, tending the kitchen and the mending. Pah!" Grania spat on the ground. "When I heard that Dónal was slain, I gathered as many men as I could find and force marched to Castlekirk before the Joyces could arrive. If the Joyces thought that Dónal did well defending the castle, they learned a harder lesson when they tried to attack Granuaile."

"So what happened?" Molly asked.

Grania's smile was wicked. "What happened was that the Joyces were routed by our defenses. After that the Joyces renamed the castle Hen's Castle."

Molly burst into laughter, holding her stomach. "Oh, that's so *funny!* I mean — not the part about Dónal getting killed, but — renaming Cock's Castle to Hen's Castle. They thought they could get the best of you because you're a woman, but they ended up respecting you more than Dónal, even though he was a fighter his whole life!"

Grania grinned. "The Joyces didn't underestimate me after that!" She glanced up at the sun. "Look at the time! El, you and I need to get some things done today, and Edmund needs to get back to Burrishoole. Molly, I'll leave ya in Toby's charge."

"All right," Molly said. "Thank you for telling me about Hen's Castle."

Toby handed the reins of his horse to MacTibbot. "Would you mind taking King back with you since I'm staying? He'll be happier back in his own stable."

"O' course, son." Edmund MacTibbot swung easily into his own saddle, holding King's reins firmly. "C'mon, boy, let's get you back and brushed out."

Toby waved goodbye as the horses disappeared down the lane.

"Toby, y'remember where the kitchen is for lunch?" Elva's friendly eyes twinkled. "Don't let the girl starve on ye. Ye didn't see her scarf her breakfast down like I did!"

"*Who* was in a hurry this morning?" Molly grinned back at Elva. "You two go on, we'll be fine."

As Grania and Elva walked back toward the castle, Toby looked thoughtful. "What is it?" Molly asked.

"You said you wanted to know how I got my name Toby-of-the-Ships?" he replied.

Molly nodded.

"Hmmm … I was a little too young to remember the details of my birth. But I know someone who was there."

"I do, too, and she just walked off with Elva."

Toby started laughing and almost choked. "Oh, Lord, I can see why Mam likes you!" he finally wheezed. "You have the same sense of humor!"

"Are you all right?" Molly laughed. "I didn't mean for you to choke to death!"

"Come on; let's go find Myles before he forgets the story!" Toby led off toward the bay.

An older man, fit and weather-beaten, sat on a log holding a piece of rope that snaked down into a sizeable coil at his feet. The skin on his head was baked by the sun where his thinning brown hair had receded.

"Myles! Grand to find you working for a change!" Toby called out merrily.

Myles looked up and grinned. He had lost a tooth in the front, but his smile shone with pleasure. "Toby! Toby, me boy! Was that MacTibbot I saw riding off? He's kept ye busy over there at Burrishoole. I don't think I've seen ye for at least a year!"

"One reason I was fostered to MacTibbot was so I'd still be close to Mam. I've been back often enough. You've just been too busy fishing and trading and the like when I've dropped by." Toby plunked himself down on the log next to Myles. "Come sit beside me, Molly. This old codger has a story you'll want to hear."

Myles raised his eyebrows high. "Is that a fact, now? And what story would that be, Master Toby?"

"The story of how I got my name, Toby-of-the-Ships."

"Now *there's* a tale that bears retelling," the sailor agreed. "Do ye mind if I set me rope-mending aside while I enlighten this pretty young thing?"

"Careful, Molly," Toby advised. "He *is* a sailor, after all."

"Then I'm glad you thought to sit between us." Now Molly's green eyes twinkled. "Go ahead, Myles!"

"Aye, then. It was nigh on twelve years ago, and I served as a seaman on Granuaile's own galley, the *Margaret*, named after her mother. We were returning home after trading our cargo of fine Irish wool and salmon for iron, silks and red wine from Spain. Granuaile was herself great with child — *this* child." He clapped Toby on the shoulder. "She gave birth to the boy on board ship on the open sea."

"So that's why he was named Toby-of-the-Ships!" Molly exclaimed.

"Aye. But the very next day, I was on watch and spied three galleys bearin' down on us. Me blood ran cold when I saw the red flag with the turbaned image of a sultan painted on it flying from their mast."

"Who were they?" Molly asked.

"Barbary pirates from the coast o' North Africa, come to take ships and booty and slaves back to their home. They produced nothing in life, and lived only to plunder and kill."

"Did you have to fight them?"

"We had no choice. They had the favorable wind and overtook us in minutes. The devils swarmed aboard, hacking at everything with their scimitars."

"What is a scimitar?"

"*This* is a scimitar." Myles reached behind him to grasp a sword nestled in a curved leather case. The hilt gleamed with burnished silver crafted into an ornate design.

"Neat," Molly said. "But it's wider down toward the scimitar's tip. How can you get it in and out of the scabbard?"

"Look here, near the top o' the scabbard where the blade goes in. Do ye see these slits on the sides? These slits go all the way down the scabbard until they reach the point where the wide part o' the scimitar blade is. Then the scabbard's sides are solid from that part down to the tip." Myles drew the curved blade halfway from its sheath. "I've had this beauty since that fateful day. Since the day after young Toby was born at sea."

"You got this scimitar from the pirates that attacked your ship?" Molly gasped.

"I nearly died," Myles recalled softly as he slid the blade back into its holder with a click. "The pirates had the upper hand, pushing us back and back. There were too many o' them! The captain rushed down into Granuaile's cabin and I heard him beg her to come up on deck to rally the men."

"But she had just had a baby the day before!" Molly protested. "What did she do?"

Myles chuckled. "I could hear Granuaile all the way up on deck. She screamed at the captain, 'May ya be seven times worse off this day twelve months, who cannot do without me one day!' The next thing I knew she came pounding up the steps with a blanket cast about her.

"It near cost me my head, as I heard one o' the raiders just in time and ducked a slice aimed at me neck. Then Granuaile was there beside me. She raised a musket point-blank to the devil and shouted 'Take this from unconsecrated hands!' The gun roared as she fired and when the powder smoke cleared, the pirate lay dead on the deck with a hole through his chest. Granuaile stooped only to pick up his scimitar and toss it to me, saying 'Start swinging this, Myles ya worthless coward, or I'll fill your belly with steel myself!' She rallied the other men in like fashion, wading into the melee with her cutlass flashing." Myles laughed again. "We won the fight. We feared Granuaile's wrath more than the Barbary pirates!"

"And that's the same scimitar that Grania gave you?" Molly looked at the weapon in awe.

Myles drew the blade from the scabbard completely in a single fluid motion. Faint brown stains clung to the end of the curved blade. "Many a Barbary pirate tasted this edge that day. We captured their flagship and the other two galleys fled back to the African desert. There's no finer leader on the Irish seas than Granuaile, man or woman."

Toby yawned. "And I was down below, sleeping soundly through all of that."

Myles scowled at him. "Ye were screaming in fear the whole time from all o' the commotion. I had to change your diaper twice to get back into your mother's good graces."

"See, Molly, I told you we'd get a better story if Myles told it." Toby winked at her and elbowed the sailor.

"Well, I'd best be getting back to mendin' this rope or the *Margaret* is going to float away." Myles grinned broadly as he picked up the coiled hemp. "It's grand to see ye again, Toby!"

Toby and Molly walked toward the shoreline and Croagh Patrick in the distance. Dozens of low islands in Clew Bay rose from the water to their right. Clare Island lay in the distance, her craggy hilltops smoky in the morning haze.

"Your mother is really something, Toby," Molly said. "I mean it. She's had more adventures than I could imagine!"

"You're right," Toby nodded, "but she's not shy about keeping to tradition when it suits her. In fact, I have to tell you another story about just that."

Molly nodded, eager to hear another tale about this remarkable woman. She noticed something a little bit different as Toby began, though. *Something in his voice? Why does this seem odd all of a sudden?* An uneasy feeling settled over her and would not go away.

"Mam was preparing to return home after a successful trading trip to Dublin a few years back. They needed a place to stay for the night and get a good meal. She went up to Castle Howth to request a meal and bed from Lord Howth, the Gaelic chieftain there."

"Grania really expected to get all of that from a stranger? I don't get it." Molly frowned.

"In Gaelic society, hospitality is supremely important," Toby explained patiently. "But Granuaile found the door closed and barred. Lord Howth sent a servant to inform his visitors that the family was at supper and could not be disturbed. What Lord Howth did was inconsiderate and rude. For a single night, a good Gaelic lord will entertain even his worst enemy to fulfill his duties of being a hospitable host!"

"So what did Grania do? Storm the castle?"

"She thought seriously about it. But then she found a young man walking outside the castle walls. Turned out he was Lord Howth's grandson himself. Mam took him with her to the ships and sailed immediately for home."

Molly's jaw dropped. "She *kidnapped* him?"

"Aye. It's quite common, really. Most of the time the hostage is held for ransom or is kept to ensure the family won't attack the clan holding the hostage. In this case, Lord Howth had to make the trip across Ireland and ask Mam what ransom she demanded for the release of his grandson."

"I suppose as a pirate, she demanded a lot of gold or weapons?" Molly asked.

Toby smiled. "That's what Lord Howth thought at first. But Granuaile told him that the ransom was to be that forever afterward, Castle Howth would have its doors open to visitors and there would always be an extra plate set at their table to welcome strangers."

"Awesome! I've never met anyone like your mother before!" Molly tried to smile, but the uncomfortable thought crept back into her head: *Something is not right here. What am I missing?*

Toby stopped and turned to face the red-haired girl, his arms crossed. "And I've never met anyone like you before, Molly." His eyes were no longer laughing, but deadly serious.

"W-What do you mean, Toby?"

"Mam thought there was something different about you, and she asked me to try to find out what it is."

"Oh — so that's what she was whispering to you when Elva and I walked up." Molly nervously clasped her hands behind her. "Did you find out?"

"I think so. As part of my fosterage, I study many things. One of those things is English. The English are moving into Ireland, and I'm going to have to be able to speak and understand their language."

"Okay, but I don't understand what — "

"Molly, Granuaile understands enough English to get by if she has to, but she speaks Irish. She *thinks* in Irish, or Gaelic if you prefer. Do you understand yet?"

Molly shook her head. "No."

"When Granuaile told you the story of Hen's Castle, she told it in Irish. When you asked questions or said anything, you spoke in English. Granuaile's speaking in Irish, you're speaking in English, *and no one even notices this?*"

Molly clasped her hands in front of her now. "I don't know, maybe, Grania was busy thinking about the story and didn't notice since she understands English anyway?"

"Unlikely, but possible. Can you guess why I had Myles tell the story of how I got my name?"

Molly felt her stomach knot up. *This is not good.* "Um, because he was there?"

"Nice try. It's because Myles *speaks only Irish.*"

"And, that's odd because no one notices anything?"

"I knew you were a smart girl. Myles understood what you were saying as clear as anything, even though you were speaking English. And just as interesting, you understood everything that Myles was saying, even though he was speaking Irish. Now why would you speak English if you understand Irish?"

Molly sighed. "Go on. Now tell me why you told the story of Howth Castle."

"Do you want to guess why I did that?"

Molly closed her eyes and took a deep breath. "Did you tell that story in English?"

"Bravo!" Toby exclaimed, clapping his hands in celebration. "But that doesn't explain everything, does it? You're not sure if you're hearing Irish or English, while everyone around understands you no matter what language *they* speak."

He stepped closer and Molly looked deeply into his crystal blue eyes. They were serious, but not menacing. The corner of his mouth turned up just enough to suggest a smile lurking there. "Molly O'Malley, what secrets are you hiding from me?"

chapter five

Secrets between Friends

"I wish you wouldn't use my whole name like that. That's what my mom does when she's mad at me." Molly sighed and pushed her hair back over her ears. "You're right, though. It's time I shared some secrets. I've been dying to tell someone, but I wasn't sure who I could trust."

"And now you trust me?" Toby looked doubtful.

"No, not really. Don't misunderstand me, I think you're great, and your mom is totally awesome, but really, what reason do I have to trust you?"

"I *did* trick you," he admitted. "That probably doesn't boost your confidence in me."

"It was a pretty neat trick, actually. Now you know that something strange is going on, and I can't hide it any more. So whether I trust you or not, I need to explain — at least as much as I know."

"This sounds like it could get complicated. Let's find a shady spot to sit down."

"I like that plan. And you're right, it *is* complicated."

They found some flat stones under a towering oak tree where they made themselves comfortable. Molly crossed her legs under her and wriggled up against the rough trunk. "It's always hardest in the beginning when two people learn to trust each other. At least, that's the way it was with Paddy and me," she said.

"Who's Paddy?"

"He's the reason I'm in this mess now, at least ultimately. If it weren't for Paddy, I wouldn't have gotten the medallion." She pulled the carved stone disk hung on the gold chain from under her shirt. "This is the reason I can understand Irish. It's magic."

"Magic?" Toby looked doubtful. "And you got this medallion from Paddy?"

"No, I got the medallion from a dragon. Don't give me that look, now, we're just getting started."

"All right, then, we'll do it your way. You got the medallion from a *dragon?*"

Molly sighed. "I guess I'd better start at the beginning, or you're never going to be able to keep up. There's so much that has happened. It all started last summer when I went to Ireland to stay with my aunt, and I met Paddy."

Toby frowned. "I thought Mam said you didn't have any family."

"I'm coming to that. Anyway, I met Paddy, and he was suspicious of me at first until we talked and began to trust each other."

"Why was Paddy suspicious?"

"Because he's a leprechaun, silly, and they're generally suspicious of 'big 'uns' as they call us. Oh, sorry, I guess I didn't mention that he was a leprechaun."

Toby's mouth hung open, but no words came out.

"Okay, you just listen then, and if you think of any questions later, let me know. So, where was I? Oh, yes, the leprechauns had a problem. Something was stealing their gold. So I told Paddy it was all right to grant me three wishes to help the leprechauns find the thief."

Toby found his voice, strained as it was. "A leprechaun gave you three *wishes?*"

"Yep. I promised to use them only to help the leprechauns. I used the first wish to find the thief. The thief turned out to be a black dragon. Fire-breathing, no less."

"Uh-huh."

"Well, we couldn't very well take on a full-grown dragon by ourselves, so I used the second wish to solve the problem of the black dragon."

"And you got rid of the dragon?"

"Well, not exactly. It made a white dragon appear."

"You really don't have much good luck with wishes, do you?"

"Ha ha. The white dragon was named Stanley, and he was a perfect gentleman, thank you very much. Oh, and he breathed ice instead of fire."

"Ah. Balance. Opposition. Something that could fight the fire-breathing dragon. Did they destroy each other?"

"Of course not. They fell in love and went back to Ellesyndria together."

Toby shook his head. "Molly, you're going to have to slow down. What is Ellesyndria?"

"Oh, I forgot that part. My second wish summoned Stanley from the land of Ellesyndria, another dimension where the dragons live safely. They were all sent there in the year 1317 by Morubek — he's a magic-user who loved the dragons — so they wouldn't be hunted to extinction here on Earth. All except Nefra."

"Who is Nefra?"

Molly stopped to catch her breath. "Nefra is the black dragon. Well, almost black, she has a blue stripe that runs down each side from front to back. She missed going to Ellesyndria because she wasn't hatched yet. She grew up all by herself until we found her again."

"Molly, do you realize how crazy this all sounds?"

Molly stood up and put her fists on her hips. "Look, buster, you're the one who wanted to know what secrets I was hiding from you. Now I'm spilling my guts here, and I'm trying to do the best I can. Do you want to hear the rest of it or not?"

"I'm sorry, I'm sorry," Toby said softly, motioning her to sit down. "I'll listen. Go on."

Molly sat down again and took a deep breath. "Toby, I haven't even gotten to the crazy part yet. I used the third wish to send Stanley and Nefra to Ellesyndria where they would be safe. Before she left, Nefra gave me this medallion. Nefra was using it to talk with us, because she only spoke Irish. She didn't need it any more because she could use dragon-talk to speak with the other dragons in Ellesyndria."

"You're right. That sounds perfectly normal. When do we get to the crazy part?"

"Coming up now. Paddy gave me a magic coin that I could use to take me to Ireland just by pulling it out of a pouch, and return home by putting it back into the pouch."

"Convenient."

"I went to see him, using the coin, and found him in prison awaiting sentencing for stealing a coin from the Fairy Queen. You can guess which coin that was."

Toby couldn't suppress a grin. "I think I like this Paddy. Can I meet him?"

"I don't think so. He's not going to be born for another, oh, twenty-nine years or so."

Toby's smile vanished. "How do you know that?"

"This is where it starts getting crazy. I tried to rescue Paddy from prison by bringing him back home with me, but there was a problem. The coin was enchanted to bring me to Paddy. When I tried to use the coin to transport Paddy, too, the coin got 'confused' and took us both to Glimmer."

"What in the heck is Glimmer?"

"It's a place where ideas become real. All of the fairy-folk get their power from there. It's beautiful, but it can be scary, too. While we were there, we kept shifting through time, mostly backwards."

"I take it you got back somehow?"

"Yes, with the help of a young woman in the Fairy Queen's court named Lioc. Lioc had the power to guide us to the right time. A rock nymph named Sandy helped us get to the right place. She could transport between one rock and another. Together they got us back to our own world and our own time."

"So what's the problem now?"

"My parents, my aunt, and I were touring Ireland, and we went to Rockfleet. When we were in Grania's bedroom, I noticed a carving on the wall that matched the pattern of Nefra's medallion *exactly*. I went over to it to compare them more closely, and I must have touched them together. When I did that, I found myself in the room with your mom, and there was a fire, and furniture, and the carving on the wall was gone. The only thing I can figure is that somehow it happened again."

"What happened again?"

Molly sighed. "I must be back in Glimmer. That's the only reasonable explanation I can think of. *Please* tell me you know about Glimmer."

Toby leaned back and stretched, shaking his head as if trying to absorb everything. "It's as I told you, I don't know anything about Glimmer." His eyes suddenly lit up with new understanding. "Molly, you haven't told me what year you're *really* from."

She gulped. "In my time, Rockfleet is an abandoned castle, empty but still standing. Grania is a figure in our history books. Ireland …"

Toby leaned forward, grabbed her shoulders and shook her slightly. "Molly, *what year?*"

Molly looked into Toby's clear blue eyes, her lip quivering. "More than four hundred years in your future."

He released her and swayed backward, breathing heavily.

"Toby, the reason I wanted to go to Donegal is because I wanted to find King Finvarra who rules the fairies now. I knew him as Fionn when I was in Glimmer. If anyone can help me get back home, he can. Castle Tiarnach is the royal fairy palace there."

Toby stared at her in shock. "I don't believe you," he whispered.

"I know," she replied softly. "But you *must* believe in the medallion. You're the one who proved that it worked. I didn't even know that I couldn't tell the difference when someone was speaking Irish or English. The medallion proves that I'm telling you the truth."

He nodded. "Don't be angry with me, it still sounds crazy. I believe that *you* believe what you are saying. You seem sincere. I just can't accept it, that's all."

Molly stretched her hand out and laid it on his. "Well, at least you know my secrets now." Toby managed to exhale deeply, and they smiled together.

They rose to walk back to the castle. As they picked their way along the shore, Molly thought: *Yes, Toby, you know about everything now ... except for the magic cloth that Queen Meb, the Fairy Queen, gave me. After all, a girl has to have some secrets.*

chapter six

Two Birds

Molly and Toby visited the kitchen, filling their plates with spiced chicken, carrots with the green part still attached, and soft brown rolls. Toby balanced two mugs of milk as they found a table outside.

"Best we don't get in the way of refurbishing the castle," Toby advised as he munched a carrot. "Mam's got everyone available busy restocking everything. Elva did a good job of keeping the living areas together while Mam was in prison. It's the armory that's getting the real workover."

Molly looked out over the bay as she tore off pieces of chicken with her fingers. The sun was high overhead, almost noon now. She was grateful for the occasional puffy cloud that drifted overhead, blocking the heat for a few minutes as the cool breeze blew in across the water. Then something on the far side of the bay captured her attention. "Toby, what's that?"

Lights on Clare Island flashed rapidly, over and over. Toby frowned as he squinted to see. "There's a galley, just coming into the bay from the south. Why is Clare signaling?"

Now a thin blue thread of smoke spiraled up from the island, growing thicker and darker by the second. "Something's wrong. Something's *very* wrong." Toby stood up quickly, leaving his lunch plate on the table. "Come on, Molly!"

The two ran across the space to Rockfleet Castle, where Granuaile was already shouting orders at everyone within earshot. She saw Toby and Molly approaching and sprinted to meet them.

"Toby," she said, "we're under attack. There's a large English fleet pursuing the galleys. The sentries on Clare Island estimate twenty ships. We've got to get supplies and defenders into the castle and scatter the rest o' the people inland."

"Do you want me to help get people to Burrishoole?"

Granuaile bit her lip briefly as she looked out toward Clare Island. A second galley rounded the point, oars dipping rhythmically into the water. "No. I have a special task for ya."

"What is it?"

"I need ya to sail out on the *Margaret*. Take the galleys and a couple o' baggage ships to the O'Donnell." She paused, her eyes darkening to midnight blue, matching the shade of the water as another cloud lingered overhead. "Bring the gallowglass. Three hundred if ya can pry that many away from old Hugh."

Toby's eyes widened. "Me?"

"Yes, you. Take Molly with ya, there's not enough food in the castle as it is. She'll be safer on board."

"B-But Mam, are you sure ..."

Granuaile whirled on her son like the leading edge of a storm. "I don't have time for this! You'll go as my personal representative! Caleb will be there if ya must have a nanny. Now go! We both have work to do!" With that she swept off toward the castle, bellowing commands non-stop as she went.

Toby remained rooted in place, staring blankly after his mother until Molly shook his arm. "Toby! Toby, I think this is serious! You should do as your mother says!"

Toby blinked and shook his head. "Yes. Yes, we must get to the *Margaret*. Let's go." He led the way along the shore, running toward the dark-hulled vessel resting on the sand nearby. Molly glanced over her shoulder to catch the unlikely sight of two men trotting toward Rockfleet carrying a half-roasted boar between them on a spit, the meat still steaming from the kitchen fire.

The galley's blunt prow thrust deeply onto the shore. Sailors lent strong hands to hoist them onto the wood-planked deck. A half-dozen men jumped into the shallow water and pushed the front of the boat as the oars near the rear came to life, splashing from back to front to pull the galley clear. The long boat slid smoothly into the water far more quickly than Molly would have expected, and the men climbed back aboard, trailing wet footprints as they returned to their stations.

"Master Bourke!" A raven-haired man in short trousers and a leather vest over his shirt padded up in his bare feet. "What's going on?"

"Caleb," Toby sighed with relief and grasped his arm. "We need to lead the other galleys to the O'Donnell, pick up some baggage ships along the way. We're to fetch the gallowglass."

Caleb gave a low whistle. "Granuaile must be expectin' *some* fight." He nodded at Molly. "Introductions later, young Toby. We'll get underway immediately." He moved away, barking orders as the ship made for deeper water.

"Watch your step, Molly," Toby advised. "The deck can get slippery, and once we're moving, it doesn't stay level. I'd recommend taking your shoes off so you don't fall."

Molly looked around and saw that all of the sailors were indeed barefoot. She slipped off her flats and shoved them into her backpack-purse. Toby pulled off his own shoes and started toward the back of the ship. "I'm going to try to find some trews that fit me," he called over his shoulder as he entered the round-topped cabin. "I'm on board often enough that we usually keep *something* my size in the trunk."

"What are trews?" she asked as she followed him. She steadied herself against the mast as the galley lurched, turning away from Rockfleet.

"They're the pants that everyone's wearing that come down just below the knee," he answered from inside the cabin. "You're wearing trews now. Ah, here's a pair that's close enough. I'll be out in just a minute."

Molly looked out across the bay. Several islands were scattered along the shallow shoreline where Rockfleet guarded the coast. The galley slipped to the north side of these islands, keeping them between the *Margaret* and the approaching fleet.

"There, that's better," Toby announced as he stepped onto the deck. "The fine clothes are great when it's cold out, but tights are too slippery on a ship's deck. I'll pack them away for when we reach the O'Donnell." His brown trews were a little baggy on him, but he had rolled up the legs to sag just below his knees. He left his white shirt open at the collar.

"Where's the English fleet?" Molly asked.

"Hopefully clear across the bay," he growled. "You might catch a glimpse of them as we clear this island. We should be able to relax a little now. We can only row so fast."

The banks of oars dipped into the water in unison, moving the galley forward smoothly. One sailor held a small drum that looked like a large tambourine without the bells. He played a soft, steady drumbeat with a stick in time with the oars. "What kind of drum is that?" asked Molly.

"That's a *bodhrán*," Toby replied. "The beat helps the rowers pull their oars at the same time. He's keeping it quiet now so the sound doesn't carry too far over the water. We're trying to sneak away, you know."

"Yeah, I got that. Oh, look! There they are!" She pointed at a large cluster of ships rounding the point between the southern shore of Clew Bay and Clare Island. The ships had several tall masts each, with billowing white sails. More sails were being hauled into place as they entered the bay, and Molly could see bold red crosses on the largest square sails.

"They're catching the favorable wind now. It was against them coming north. That's what slowed them down, they had to tack."

"Tack?"

"They had to sail at angles to the wind, and zigzag back and forth. That's tacking. Tacking takes more time because you have to travel farther and it's not as efficient as having the wind directly behind you."

"Why aren't we using our sails?" Molly looked up at the galley's canvas scrunched tight against the yard crosspiece high up on the mast.

"One, the wind is against us right now. It would slow us down rather than help us go faster. Two, using the sail would make it easier for the English to see us. By leaving the sail furled, there's not as much to see." Toby looked across the water at the unwelcome invaders. "We have the advantage with a galley. We can row against the wind. Their ships have no oars, so they have to rely on the wind completely."

The *Margaret* slipped past the last islet toward the north side of Clare Island. The other two galleys from Granuaile's fleet had turned back toward Clare Island and the Atlantic Ocean rather than be trapped in the bay by the huge English fleet. The three galleys moved closer together as they continued along the coastline.

Black cliffs bordered their right side as they hugged the shore. "That's Corraun," Toby said. "We're coming up to Achill Island next."

"We were going to go there," Molly whispered to herself. "In the car."

The galleys slowed as they approached the inlet that separated Achill Island from the Irish mainland. As the *Margaret* turned to the north, the other two galleys took up positions watching the English ships bear down on Rockfleet at the other end of Clew Bay. Molly could see puffs of white smoke appear from the decks of the attacking ships and answering puffs from the direction of the castle. A sound like firecrackers at a great distance echoed in her ears; distant thunder erupting from each new white cloud. She turned her attention to the inlet as the Margaret approached a square stone tower ahead on the left bank.

Two sailing vessels, one a bit larger than the other, lay quietly at anchor in the inlet, but their decks bristled with activity. Sails hung on poles were already being winched up, stretched into place by ropes and pulleys and held at sloping angles. The larger vessel raised a single triangle-shaped sail on the rear-most of its three masts.

A man on the smaller vessel waved at the galley as they neared. "What are orders, sir?" he called through cupped hands.

"We're going to Tyrconnell. We'll need every spare hold you've got." Caleb pointed back toward the bay. "I think we can get safely away if we move quickly."

The other man nodded. "We saw. We'll be ready in a few minutes." He turned back to his sailors who began hoisting a chain from the water. The anchor broke the surface, the smooth iron glistening as rivulets of water ran off.

The *Margaret* turned smartly about in the channel, her oars moving in opposite directions on each side. The sailing boats followed slowly behind them as the crews struggled to adjust the triangular sails. The larger sails on the bigger ship remained tightly furled on the yards of her front masts.

"Why don't they use all of their sails?" Molly asked.

Toby cast a quick look over his shoulder. "The wind is from the north. The square sails are generally more of a hindrance when sailing into the wind. That's why we use the lateen sails — the triangle shaped ones — to catch the wind at an angle."

"And tack into the wind." Molly nodded. "I remember. But why are we taking sailing ships if galleys can travel more easily into the wind?"

"Did you hear Caleb say we're going to need every hold they've got?"

"Yes."

"Look at our galley. It's long and narrow. It has to be lightweight so it can be rowed through the water. But it doesn't have a lot of storage space below decks. Plus, we can't build structures too high above decks, or it gets top heavy and could tip over. That's what happened with Henry the Eighth's ship, the *Mary Rose,* although that was a sailing ship itself — the English built additional top decks on the ship that were loaded with armored soldiers and cannon. The *Mary Rose* tipped over too far during a battle with the French while making a turn, and water came in through the lower gun ports. She foundered and sank, of course."

"I'm confused. Which are better, galleys or sailing ships?"

"Sailing ships can be built higher and deeper than galleys, because they don't rely on human power to move them. They can take long ocean journeys more easily, because rowers get tired, and you have to carry more food and water for a large crew of rowers. The biggest difference is that sailing ships can carry more weight, so you can mount larger cannon. As guns get bigger, the sailing ship is going to become the warship of choice. But we're taking our sailing ships with us today because we need them to carry a lot of cargo."

"I wanted to ask you about that. Grania said you're supposed to get the gallowglass? What's that?"

Toby smiled. "The gallowglass are Scottish mercenaries. Granuaile often ferries them down to fight for one lord or another in conflicts we have. This time she intends to use them for herself, to drive off the English. It's ironic, though."

Molly frowned. "What do you mean, ironic?"

"We're killing two birds with one stone. Some of the gallowglass live in Ireland — the O'Donnell lets them stay on his land. So while our main mission is to bring back the gallowglass to help Granuaile in this battle, you're going to get your wish, too."

"What wish?"

"The O'Donnell lives in Donegal. Didn't you say that you wanted to go there?"

chapter seven

Celtic Conundrum

What? We're going to Donegal?"

Toby smiled smugly. "Don't blame me. It's the blasted English that forced us to — whoa!"

Molly threw her arms around his neck and planted a kiss on his cheek. "Oh, thank you, thank you! I was beginning to think I'd *never* get home!"

"Wait, Molly, there's no need to — oh, hello, Caleb."

Molly loosened her grip and turned to see the *Margaret's* captain, standing with his arms crossed and sporting a huge grin on his face. "Well, Master Toby, do you have time for that introduction now?"

Toby cleared his throat and carefully removed Molly's arms from his neck. "Uh, Caleb, this is Molly O'Malley. She's here as a guest of Mam's. I guess this is some welcome. Molly, meet Captain Caleb MacNally."

"Aye, some welcome indeed!" The captain winked broadly.

"I meant the English attack! And — and she kissed *me* just now! I only met her this morning!" Toby flushed scarlet as he smoothed his shirt collar.

"Only this mornin', now? Very good work, Master!"

"*Caleb!* She's just excited about going to Donegal! She — has some friends up there ... so she says." Toby glared at Molly who did her best to smile back.

"Really? Some o' the clan O'Donnell? O'Neill?" Caleb appeared interested.

"Well, let's just say I know some people in high places, if I can find their castle," Molly offered.

"And what castle would that be, milady?"

"Castle Tiarnach."

Caleb frowned. "Never heard of it."

"I've heard of it." They all turned to the speaker, an older man, slightly balding, wearing a grey wool sweater.

"Myles!" Molly shouted with delight.

He chuckled at the outburst. "I've heard o' the place, but you'll ne'er find it. It's the home o' the fairy king. No mortal can find it unless the fairies want them to."

"Well, how do you know they don't want me to find it?" Molly pouted and propped her fists on her hips.

"If ye truly know people — or fairies — in high places, then ye might find it. Are they expectin' ye, then?"

Molly's face fell. "Not exactly."

Myles became serious. "It's not a lark to be meetin' the fairy folk. Many a soul's been lost trying to find them. If ye survive one encounter, that should be quite enough. Ye'll gain a story that can be retold for the rest o' your life."

"Yeah, if I can find anyone who believes me." Molly glared at Toby, who shifted nervously.

Caleb spoke up. "We're going to Donegal, but only to the coast. I know the area well, and I don't think the castle you're looking for is nearby. If ye don't know where it lies to begin with, ye may have trouble findin' it, fairy curse or no."

"Well, I've got to try." A single tear trickled slowly from Molly's eye. She gently wiped it away.

"We'll do everything we can, Molly," Toby whispered.

Molly smiled and brushed her hair back. "So, Myles, what do you do on this ship?"

"I'm the navigator. I'm too old for the oars, but still young enough to remember where the islands are!" He winked at her.

"I'm glad there's someone else on board that I know. And it was nice to meet you, too, Captain MacNally."

"We're generally on a first-name basis on board Granuaile's ships, Miss. Caleb will do."

"Then please call me Molly instead of 'Miss.' I'm not used to titles, either!"

The little fleet sailed along Achill Island's southwest coast as Myles and Caleb returned to their duties. Molly noted that the galleys now pulled lateen sails into place that billowed out in the breeze.

"I thought we couldn't use sails?" Molly asked.

Toby glanced at the canvas stretched in front of the mast. "The baggage ships must tack now anyway, so we may as well use what wind we can. The galleys have both a lateen sail and a square sail. We use the lateen sail to get an extra push going into the wind. When the wind blows from behind us, we'll put up the square sail. Do you want to know the ships' names?"

"Sure!"

"The darker-colored galley is the *Black Oak,* named after Mam's father. The other galley with the lighter colored hull is the *Sea Witch.* The *Sea Witch* is one of the original galleys that Mam brought with her when she came back to Umhall and Clare Island after Dónal was killed. It's originally an O'Flaherty ship, manned by O'Flahertys who would rather follow Mam than stay with their own clansmen. The O'Flahertys have been seafarers like the O'Malleys for generations."

"What are the sailing ships called?"

"The smaller one is the *Banshee.* It's a caravel, with two masts and all lateen sails. She has a shallower draft, so she can travel in water that's not as deep, farther up rivers and so on. The Portuguese invented them to be used as their primary exploring vessels."

"And the bigger one?"

"That's the *Trident*. It's a carrack. It has three masts and is slower than the *Banshee*, but it carries more cargo. It uses square sails except on the mizzen-mast."

"Is that the mast closest to the back?"

Toby nodded. "Yes. The back is called the stern on a ship. The carrack can't travel as quickly against the wind as a caravel, but with a wind behind it, the square sails will make up the difference in speed. The *Trident* is just our cargo ship, though. When we have to fight, we rely on the *Banshee*. We have a cannon mounted on the forecastle of the *Banshee*, because she's more maneuverable."

"I keep thinking I've seen sailing ships like these before. I'm trying to remember where. You said the caravel was invented by the Portuguese?"

"Yes, but everyone uses them. The Spanish used them early on, but they are starting to use more galleons now. A galleon is a larger, faster ship than the carrack, used to bring back trading goods from the New World."

"That's it!" Molly cried. "The Spanish! Didn't Columbus discover America for the Spanish? What kind of ships did he have?"

"You're talking about Christopher Columbus? The man who discovered the New World? Let me think." Toby frowned as he searched his memory. "We trade with Spain on a regular basis, but they keep their maps pretty close, almost a secret. Let's see, Columbus' ships — I believe he had two caravels and a carrack. You've seen them?"

"No, not the ships themselves, but pictures that artists have drawn. It was, um, the Nina, the Pinta, and the Santa Maria!" she finished proudly.

"That would be right. The Santa Maria was the largest of the three; it was the carrack."

Molly was silent for a minute as they watched the waves roll by. The oars broke the water's surface in smooth harmony, leaving a white froth behind until they plunged into the dark sea once more.

"I'm sorry. I didn't mean to embarrass you earlier," Molly blurted out. "I was only ..."

"As I said, you were happy to be going to Donegal," Toby smiled, his blue eyes twinkling. "You surprised me, you didn't embarrass me. *Caleb* embarrassed me."

Molly suppressed a giggle. "He wasn't going to let up on you! Are you two good friends?"

"I know all of the crew well enough. I've been on board Mam's ships since before I was born." He grinned. "Caleb and I get along well enough."

"You said this morning that MacTibbot is your foster father. Why do you have a foster father if Grania is around to take care of you? Why would your real mother give you up like that?"

Toby shook his head and sat down on the deck. "You're loaded up with more questions than Clew Bay has islands. Have a seat."

Molly sat down beside him and he continued. "In Gaelic society, Irish ruling families like mine follow the tradition of sending their children to live with a foster parent. The foster parent is usually a sub-chief of the family. This helps build stronger ties between the rulers and those who serve under them. In the foster home the child generally has all the benefits as if he or she was a natural child. MacTibbot is dear to me, and he treats me like his own son."

Molly nodded. "I think I understand. When my dad sent me to Ireland to live with my aunt Shannon, I sort of felt like a foster child. My aunt and I grew much closer while I was there. Even my dad wound up getting closer to Aunt Shannon. I guess that's like the ruling family getting closer to the sub-chief in your world."

"I think you've got it." He sighed, looking out at the other ships. "My world may soon disappear, though."

"What do you mean?"

"It's the English. The Tudors who rule England are plotting to reconquer Ireland. They're doing it smart, though. Instead of sending armies over to invade, they're using the strategy of 'surrender and re-grant.' So far, it seems to be working."

"What is 'surrender and re-grant?'"

"We Irish have our own titles of nobility and leadership. For example, you've heard me talk about the O'Donnell. That's a title of leadership for the O'Donnell clan. The leader elected to the position also gets property to use and may collect tributes from the other lords while he holds the title. In my family, it's called the MacWilliamship. The titles are inherited to some extent, but the leaders are elected by the other nobles in the clan based on the leaders' abilities and the nobles' respect for them. The English want to change all of that. They don't want independent lords running Eire."

"So who surrenders?"

"The Irish lord surrenders all of his titles and possessions to the English crown. In return, the Crown grants an English title and gives all of the lands back to him."

"And then the English leave them alone?"

"Hardly," Toby smirked. "Once the lord submits, he is under the power of the English crown. He goes to meet with the Tudor authority as an independent Gaelic chieftain, and returns an indentured English knight. He must pay taxes to England, provide armies for battle on their behalf, and follow English law and customs."

"Does it make that much difference whether you're an Irish lord or an English lord?"

"It can. Mam's first husband, Dónal, was *tanaiste* to the highest chieftain of the O'Flaherty clan."

"The understudy?"

"Hmmm. I forgot that you understand Irish. Yes, *tanaiste* means 'understudy,' meaning he's been selected to be next in line for the highest post. A *tanaiste* can be a brother, a cousin, a nephew — whoever is best qualified to lead."

"That sounds reasonable."

"But under English law, it's always the eldest son that inherits everything. It doesn't matter if the son can't find his way out of an outhouse, he'll still be the next leader."

"Then why would anyone agree to the surrender and re-grant?"

"One of the minor lords in the O'Flaherty clan, Murrough of the Battle Axes, realized he was never going to get the support he needed to become the next leader. He surrendered his Gaelic title, which didn't amount to much in the first place, and the English appointed him ruler over all of Ian-Chonnacht. Just like that, Dónal's right to the title of the O'Flaherty was stolen."

Molly's jaw dropped. "How could the English just appoint someone to rule like that? They're not even from Ireland."

"No, but they have soldiers and ships, and most importantly they think of themselves as a nation. Englishmen fight together for England and for Queen Elizabeth. In Ireland, every Gaelic lord fights for power for himself, so they end up fighting each other, even inside the same clan. The English are taking advantage of that. By setting up Murrough of the Battle Axes as ruler, the other Gaelic lords started fighting him instead of fighting the English."

"That's so sneaky." Molly frowned and pondered her bare feet. "Did Dónal fight back?"

"He never got the chance. He died soon afterward. The Hen's Castle story, remember?"

"Oh, yeah. So this surrender and re-grant is really a big deal, then?"

"It's the main English policy. It's cheaper than sending soldiers to fight. Let the Irish fight each other."

"Why are they attacking your mother, then?"

Toby sighed and ran his fingers through his curly blond hair. "I don't know. Mam was released from Dublin prison, we don't know why. No one has ever escaped from Dublin prison. Most prisoners are executed. MacTibbot thinks they may have released her so she could persuade my father to stop attacking the English and their allies."

"Would she do that?"

"She'd more likely turn the gallowglass over to him to use after she's through with them."

"Wow, she loves him that much?"

"More because *he'd* have to pay them for their services and she wouldn't have to."

They both laughed until their sides hurt. "Toby," Molly finally gasped, "are your mom and dad still married? I thought Grania dismissed your father from the walls of Rockfleet castle."

"That she did. My father understands Mam's need for independence, though. It's like a secret game between them. No one controls Mam, and he doesn't try to. They support each other for the most part, but they still disagree sometimes."

"Okay, tell me more about where we're going. I want to know as much as possible so I can find Castle Tiarnach when we get there."

Toby shook his head. "We can ask the O'Donnell, but he probably doesn't have any more idea where it is than Caleb does. Look, I know you want to run off into the woods and find a group of friendly fairies waiting to greet you with open arms, but there's not going to be anyone available to take you on a long trip. Our job is to get the gallowglass and return to

Rockfleet as fast as we can. You saw the guns firing. Mam's in a battle for her life." He ended quietly, almost as if he was talking to himself.

"I'm sorry. I don't mean to sound like I don't care about Grania. Of course I'll help you get the gallowglass. But it's really important for me to try and find the fairy kingdom again. It's going to be *my* only chance."

He looked into her green eyes. "Myles believes in the fairies, too. Most people don't pay too much attention to that side of him; he's a fine navigator and a loyal soldier and sailor. But Myles has never actually seen a fairy, and he never will. We'll be in Donegal for a few days and you can search during that time, but you must be prepared to return with the gallowglass."

"You still don't get it," Molly sighed. "I *have* seen fairies. My best friend is a leprechaun. It's not my fault that *you* haven't seen any."

Toby chuckled. "I'll grant you that. I've heard that help from the fairies is not always what you expect or want. Hugh O'Donnell isn't relying on fairies, at any rate."

"Is he the O'Donnell you keep talking about?"

"Yes. Between him and the O'Neill, they're pushing hard to get all Eire to band together and throw the English out."

"Well, why don't you?"

Toby shook his head. "Because for the most part, the Irish are only looking out for themselves, not for Ireland. It's survival first. Only a few years ago Mam offered the English Lord Deputy, Sir Henry Sidney, three galleys and two hundred fighting men whenever he needed them."

Molly felt her jaw drop again. "Grania submitted to the English?"

"No," Toby smiled. "She moved first to keep the English from seeing her as an enemy. She sailed to Galway

City to meet with Sir Sidney and even gave him a tour of the bay on her galley."

"That was nice of her."

"She charged him for the trip."

"She didn't!"

Toby chuckled with delight. "You tell me whether or not Mam's capable of doing that. It was a rare moment for her to even *be* in Galway City. The residents don't allow O'Flahertys or O'Malleys to trade there."

"Then how do you survive?"

"We stop ships sailing into Galway and collect a portion of their cargo as a fee to guarantee their safe passage."

"You're a pirate!" Molly exclaimed.

"We're not doing anything different from what Galway City is doing on land. They collect fees to let people trade, or outlaw trading completely for clans who haven't buckled under to Elizabeth's ministers. The English have privateers — Sir Walter Raleigh and Sir Francis Drake, who prey on Spanish galleon treasure ships returning from the New World. The only difference is that they sail on behalf of a nation, and we sail for ourselves. Like I said, it's survival."

"You've got lots of problems," Molly sighed.

"Yes, it's quite a conundrum."

"A conun-what?"

"A conundrum. It's a problem or puzzle that is extremely difficult to solve."

"Where do you come up with these big words?"

"I think my Latin teacher made it up. It sounds like a fun word, though, doesn't it? Maybe it will become popular."

The three galleys, the caravel, and the carrack sailed up the coastline. Dark clouds and lightning hung off their port side, far out to sea. To Molly, it seemed as though storms were raging all over Ireland.

chapter eight

Red Hugh

The *Margaret* led Granuaile's ships into Tyrconnell harbor. Her oars splashed into the water as her mainsail tugged at the ropes, bulging with the south wind that had blessed them since the previous day.

The galleys beached themselves on the sand while the *Trident* and the *Banshee* edged close to the dock to tie up. Toby was wearing his fine clothes again and he and Molly slipped their shoes on for the first time in five days.

As they jumped onto the shore a man and a young boy approached from the nearby castle. Molly noted that the boy had red hair like hers, with just a touch of bushy-I-won't-stay-down look to it.

Toby shouted a greeting as they came near. "Hail, O'Donnell and Lord of Tyrconnell! Greetings from Grania O'Malley! Are you well?"

"Hail, Tibbot-ne-Long, prince o' Connaught!" the man answered. "I know your father doesn't care for ships all that much — is your mother with ye?"

"No, she has sent me as her representative on a crucial mission." Hugh O'Donnell's face darkened at the serious tone in Toby's voice. "Granuaile is besieged at Rockfleet by twenty English ships. She dispatched me to bring the gallowglass to help drive them away, if your soldiers are available."

"The gallowglass are always ready to drive away the English," Hugh growled. "Most are engaged in several other duties at the moment. It will take some days to recall them. How many do ye need?"

"About three hundred, my Lord."

The O'Donnell stroked his beard. "I was glad to hear o' Grania's release from prison. When I saw the flags with the O'Malley wild boar on her ships, I hoped she would be with ye. Nevertheless, the gallowglass shall be yours. 'Tis a lot o' responsibility she's handed ye, young Bourke."

"Aye. How soon can the gallowglass be ready?"

"I'll have to ask the captains. We'll send messengers immediately. In the meantime, see to your men and come to the castle when you're ready."

"Thank you. Is this little Red?"

Hugh O'Donnell nodded, and rested his hand gently on the red-haired boy's head. "I imagine he's grown a bit since ye last saw him. He'll be fostered later this summer; he's just seven this year. Red, this is Toby Bourke, and ... ?"

"Molly O'Malley, pleased to meet you," Molly piped up, deciding she should do a small curtsy under the circumstances.

Red grinned at her. "Your hair's the same color as mine!"

"Yes," Molly smiled back. "Is that how you got your name?"

He made a face. "I think so. People remember me, though."

"We'll tend to the ships and the men and meet you in a few minutes." Toby and the O'Donnell exchanged bows and turned to their respective errands.

"I can't believe how much Red's grown!" Toby exclaimed as they returned to the ships. "He was only about four the last time I saw him!"

"He's cute," Molly said. "I hope they have a great foster family for him."

"Don't underestimate him. Red Hugh is the son of a Gaelic lord, just as I am. He is quite well-educated for his age."

Toby saw to it that his captains assigned tasks to their men. He planned for necessary repairs and arranged for the servants from the O'Donnell clan to deliver fresh supplies of food and water. After setting the work shifts and scheduling the watches for the night, he said "Molly, let's see how the O'Donnell is doing with finding his gallowglass!"

They entered the castle and followed a spiral staircase up to a large hall decorated profusely with antlers. Hugh stood at the far end with Red Hugh at his side. A servant finished his conversation with the elder O'Donnell and left in haste.

"I think the messengers are all on their way now," Hugh announced. "It will probably be tomorrow before we have an answer."

"Thank you, again," Toby said. "Our ships are being resupplied and our men are being greeted warmly by the O'Donnells. While we await your messengers' return, I would ask a favor."

"Anything within my power," Hugh replied.

"Have you ever heard of a Castle Tiarnach in Donegal?"

The O'Donnell looked blankly at him for a moment. "No, I haven't. You're sure it's in Donegal?"

"Father." Red Hugh tugged gently on his father's jerkin.

"Yes, son?"

"I've heard of it."

"You have?" Molly gasped. "Do you know where it is, Red?"

He shook his bushy red curls. "I've only heard of it in stories. The bards sing about the fairy kingdom and Castle Tiarnach."

"Fairy kingdom?" The O'Donnell snorted. "Surely you've a better use o' your time than to look for mythical nonsense?"

Molly started to retort, but Toby cut her off. "It means a great deal to the girl, m'lord. I ask only a small favor, to speak with those who may have heard of this mythical place."

"Red is probably your best source for that. He spends as much time at our bard's knee listening to legends as he does at his studies." He spoke directly to his son. "Answer any questions that Toby and Molly may have. Ask for help if ye need it."

"I will, sir."

"But tonight we will feast! Toby, your men are invited to festivities at the summer kitchen, and we will all join them! But first, ye've had a tiring journey and ye need tending to. Molly, may I offer the services o' Mrs. O'Donnell and her servants? Perhaps they can find ye some clean clothes for the banquet as well."

Molly bowed again. "Thank you, my lord," she said softly. "As long as I am dressed properly to search for Castle Tiarnach tomorrow."

The O'Donnell threw back his head and roared with laughter. "And I thought there was only one female with the boldness o' Grania among the O'Malleys! Aye, search for your castle, child, while the men attend to business!" He walked off, still chuckling.

Molly felt a small, strong hand take hers. "Come on, Molly," Red Hugh urged. "I can take ye to Mam."

"Go with him," Toby smiled. "You'll feel better. It's hard being on board a ship for five days, especially for a girl."

"You've got that right," Molly responded wearily. "There's no privacy at all. I'm glad I at least had that little cabin and a chamber pot."

Molly thought it quite odd that there were no chairs at the low table set up outside the summer kitchen. At least there was a rough-sawn tree stump where she could sit in her new blue dress. It fit her nicely, and came down almost to her black flats, which as it turned out, went well with the outfit. She'd transformed her magic cloth into a slip to wear under the dress, and she still wore both her silver heart locket and Nefra's medallion around her neck.

The O'Donnell ladies had been wonderful hosts, fetching a lukewarm bath and taking her old clothes to wash, promising to return them in the morning. Molly fidgeted and looked for Red Hugh in the crowd.

She spotted him squeezing through the throng a few minutes later. He set a hunk of bread down in front of her, the loaf hollowed out and filled with steaming meat. He grinned. "Normally the food is cool by the time it goes from the kitchen to the castle. Since we're eating outside tonight, ye get your food hot!"

"What kind of meat is it?"

"Venison. There are lots of deer in the woods. Oh, here's your drink."

Molly looked at the white, creamy liquid in the wooden cup and raised an eyebrow at Red.

"It's buttermilk! Don't tell me ye don't like buttermilk! *Everyone* likes buttermilk!"

She took a sip and nodded. "You're right. I *love* buttermilk!"

The young boy beamed. "I told ye! After we eat, I'll take ye to meet Bruionn. He's our bard. He knows all the great stories like the one you're looking for."

Toby arrived and insisted that they sit at the low table with the crews from the ships. Molly saw that both Toby and she were served the meatier dishes like the O'Donnell was getting. The sailors and the servants had porridge, turnips, salads, and lots of ale to drink.

After a dessert of fruits and nuts washed down with more buttermilk, old Bruionn hobbled out, leaning on a gnarled wooden cane to entertain the company. "My Lord and honored guests! I tell you tonight a story about a Celtic king.

"There was a king named Labhras, who had a secret. Every three years he would have his hair cut, and then the king would execute his barber. Soon it was known throughout the country that it was a death sentence to cut the king's hair.

"One year a young man was selected to cut the king's hair. Reluctantly he performed the task and discovered the king's dark secret. The young man pleaded so eloquently for his life that the king agreed to spare him, on condition that he never reveal the secret to another person.

"Months passed, and the young man grew ill. A wise woman in the village told him that he harbored a great secret that wore on him, and his only hope was to tell the secret or he would perish. Although the young man was sworn to silence, he went into the woods and whispered the secret to a bay tree, thus preserving his oath to tell no person. His spirit was lifted and he felt his health return.

"Soon afterward a bard came through the same woods. He cut off a branch from that same bay tree and fashioned a beautiful harp. The next week the bard went to play for King Labhras himself, but when he strummed the harp, before the bard could utter a word, the harp shouted 'King Labhras has horses' ears! King Labhras has horses' ears!' Everyone was shocked, but o' course no one with this condition could be a king, which is why Labhras hid his ears for so long from his people.

"King Labhras had to give up his throne, and the young man who cut his hair and told the secret to the bay tree became the new king."

Molly joined in the applause. "A fine story, that!" said Toby. The O'Donnell made a point of showing everyone his normal ears and laughed uproariously. Minstrels then brought out their pipes and harps to play some lively folk tunes for the admiring sailors.

After several rousing songs, Bruionn came over to Molly and Red Hugh. "I hear ye wished to ask me a question, young Red?"

Red nodded. "Master Bruionn, can you help my friend Molly? She's trying to find Castle Tiarnach. Didn't you tell me about it once?"

"Yes, I believe I did," the old bard said. He turned his bright eyes on Molly. "Telling about it and finding it are two different things. We repeat the stories to our friends and clansmen here, but Castle Tiarnach lies only in the fairy realm."

"Yes, yes, I know, it's in Glimmer," Molly said impatiently. "That's *why* I need to get there, because I'm in Glimmer now, and I need to talk to Fionn, or King Finvarra, or whatever you call him now. He can help me get back home."

Bruionn was silent for a long time, staring intently at Molly. "So ye've been to the fairy realm, child?" he asked quietly.

"Ooh!" Molly huffed in exasperation. "Yes, I've been to the fairy realm, and somehow I'm back there again. All I want you to do is tell me how to get to Castle Tiarnach! Please!"

Bruionn's voice was gentle as he replied. "No one can lead another into the fairy realm, unless they are a fairy themself. You must find your own way there. But know this, dear child," — he leaned close to her — "we are not in the fairy world, unless my whole life has been a dream."

"Well, that's the point, isn't it? In Glimmer, ideas become real. Dreams become real. You're probably the creation of some bard who took a nap in the 16th century!" She sighed. "But even so, you have to act in harmony with the idea that made you. If you don't *believe* you can find the castle, you *won't* be able to find the castle."

The celebration continued all around them. Granuaile's sailors sipped their ale and swapped stories with the O'Donnell clan. The music played brightly across the meadow.

Red Hugh patted Molly's arm gently. "I have a dream."

Molly smiled at the boy. "Tell me."

"I want all of Ireland to unite and drive the English back to their island. The English order all of our bards to be killed because they don't want us to remember the stories and history of our people. I hate the English." Tears began to run down his face. "You take the gallowglass back to Granuaile, and make the English go away. Please, Molly?"

Molly hugged the little red-haired boy tightly, feeling her own tears start to flow. "Okay, Red. I promise. I can do that much."

chapter nine

The Gallowglass

*e*ight days! I can't believe it took eight days to get the gallowglass onto the ships! Granuaile's men would never take so long to get organized!" Toby fumed as he paced the deck of the *Margaret*.

"You think *you've* got problems! I couldn't find anyone in eight days who had any idea where Castle Tiarnach was. Five days of hiking and I didn't see one thing that looked familiar." Molly stamped her foot. "Toby, what am I going to do?"

He stopped pacing and glared at the red-haired girl. "First of all, stop whining. You're not the only one with problems. Mam is being attacked by English soldiers, we still have five ships worth o' Scottish mercenaries to insert into a battle, and the O'Donnell is not thrilled with sending his gallowglass out two months before the normal fighting season begins. If it was just another Gaelic chieftain instead of the English, I'm not sure he'd give us the soldiers at all until May. Fortunately," he let his breath hiss between his clenched teeth, "the O'Donnell hates the English and what they're doing to Eire. He'd like nothing better than for Granuaile to openly join him in revolt." Toby's mouth turned up into a crooked smile. "Maybe that's what Mam had in mind, too … a ready ally who will offer aid under difficult circumstances."

Molly stared back with her mouth open. "You people never stop scheming, do you? It's all you think about!"

"Molly, consider this. If you go home, you'll go back to a loving family and a quiet life. When I go home, I've got twenty enemy ships waiting for me, probably 200 English soldiers and a lifetime of attacks from both English and Irish alike. When I stop 'scheming,' I die."

"Okay, I get it. You've got problems. Bigger problems than I would have back home. I'd gladly face all of those problems just to *get* back home. But I can't find the castle, I can't find Fionn, and ... and I don't know if I'll *ever* get back home. I don't have anything to fight for except hope that somehow, somewhere, I'll find a way back!"

"Well, you tried for five days. Do you have any idea how crazy you sound, Miss Take-me-to-the-Fairy-Realm?"

"For the umpteenth time, we're already *in* the Fairy Realm! That bard, Bruionn, may know his stories but I know when I'm in Glimmer!" Molly's green eyes flashed.

"And you think I'm just a dream of some kind?"

"Well ... yes, I do."

"Molly, how do I know that *you're* not the one dreaming all of this up?"

"Because of the medallion and the magic cloth — oops."

Toby's eyes narrowed to slits beneath his blond locks. "*What* magic cloth?"

Molly bowed her head and shrugged. "Sorry. That just kind of slipped out, didn't it?"

"*What* magic cloth, Molly?"

She nodded toward the stern. "Let's go back to the cabin and I'll show you. I don't want everyone on board to see this."

They stepped inside the arched cabin and pulled the curtain behind them. "I'm sorry, Toby. I wasn't sure if I should tell you about the cloth. You don't believe anything else

I tell you, even though you know the medallion is magical." Molly laid her backpack-purse on the table.

"I know the medallion is strange, yes. But that doesn't mean I believe in magic."

Molly looked at him and grinned. "Then you explain this." She brushed her hand across the backpack and whispered, *"Water."*

The material shimmered for a moment, and then changed to a chocolate brown color that matched the table top. Molly slid her fingernail along the side, cutting a smooth line in the flawless cloth. She grabbed the edges and tied a knot, stretched the ends out flat, and pushed the gaps together. Then she said, *"Ice."*

"You put a bow on it," Toby said in amazement.

"Touch it. It'll stay this way until I decide to change it again. Go ahead, it's real."

He shook his blond curls. "No, it's not real. It's magic."

Molly eyed him critically. "Is it magic like you don't understand how it works, or magic like you believe me now?"

Toby sighed. "I don't think you're a magician like the ones I've seen who perform tricks. I'll take what you say more seriously from now on. This is too close, too believable to be imaginary. But I can't believe there is another world out there where fairies and leprechauns exist, much less that I'm only someone's random thought in that world."

"Fair enough," Molly nodded. "I'm just happy that you've come this far."

Toby leveled his ice-blue eyes on her. "Does this mean that you've given up finding the Fairy Realm?"

"No way! Just because I couldn't find anyone in Donegal who knew where the castle is, let alone guide me to it, doesn't mean I'm giving up. I'll just have to find another way. I'm *never* giving up."

"*That* I understand," Toby agreed. "Once you give up, you die."

"I trust Grania isn't giving up. Are these gallowglass as good as everyone says they are? Will they really be able to help when we reach Rockfleet?"

He smiled, the corner of his mouth curling up in that certain way. *That smile is starting to get to me. He's really cute,* Molly thought.

"Let's ask MacDougall. He's the ranking gallowglass commander on board. I'm sure he can give us an unbiased opinion."

Molly rolled her eyes. "Yeah, right!"

They walked to the *Margaret's* forecastle, where they found the tall Scot commander leaning on the rail, looking intently out to sea. "MacDougall?" Toby called out.

The well-muscled man responded by leaning farther over the rail and retching.

"Oh, my," Molly said.

"We've got another one," Toby sighed. He grasped MacDougall's elbow gently. "Are ye empty for the moment?"

MacDougall nodded mutely.

"Let's take you aft to the poop deck. From where you're at now, everything's going to hit all of the oars going back, and I'd rather not see that, if you know what I mean."

"You really call it a poop deck?" Molly exclaimed.

"It's not what you think," Toby replied. "Poop comes from the French word for 'stern,' *la poupe.* It simply means the highest deck on the back of the boat."

Toby led the big man to the back of the vessel to join five other gallowglass likewise adjusting to the roll of the sea. "I advise you to avoid food for a day or so. Drink lots of water, though."

"It took me a couple of days to get over my sea-sickness on the way up, but I was okay after that," Molly encouraged him.

MacDougall looked at her in amazement, and then turned to the rail again, his large frame heaving.

One of the other gallowglass at the stern rail wiped his mouth on his sleeve and laughed. "He'll be better in one day, wait and see. MacDougall will not want to be seasick longer than a wee lass!"

"Sounds like *you're* feeling better," Molly bantered. "Would you have time to answer a few questions for a 'wee lass?'"

"Aye, I think I can manage!" The soldier stumbled over to them, grabbing the railing for support as the ship plunged into a trough. "What be your pleasure?"

"What's your name, for starters?"

"Ryan Graham. I'll fight well for ye, despite me gentle disposition."

Molly nodded at Toby. "Sounding pretty confident already."

Toby laughed. "I have some doubts about his gentle disposition!"

"Yeah, me, too. Ryan, I don't want to offend you or anything, but I don't know anything about the gallowglass. Can you tell me something about yourselves?"

"Oh, let's see. We're mercenaries, professional soldiers who fight for whoever will hire us. We go all over Europe, from Ireland to France and Spain. We wear chain-mail armor, and our main battle weapons are the sword and the Great Axe. I understand we're fighting for Grania O'Malley now?"

"That's right. Do you have a problem fighting for a woman?" Molly challenged him.

Ryan guffawed loudly. "Grania has transported us to many places in Eire in years past. It's an honor to be servin' under Grania herself! She's got as much courage as that other one."

"What other one?" Molly asked.

"That woman that rules the infernal English. Elizabeth Tudor." Ryan spat over the rail.

Toby nodded. "I've heard that Elizabeth said 'I may have the body of a woman, but I have the heart and stomach of a king.' You have to respect her as a leader, even though she's tearing Eire to bits with her policies."

"Aye. We understand courage." The gallowglass soldier looked at Molly. "You're a strange sight on a ship, lass. Ye wear man's clothes like Grania is said to wear, and ye have no fear o' the gallowglass." He winked at her.

"I'm in a strange place," Molly sighed, "and I have problems of my own that are much bigger than either the English or the gallowglass."

Ryan's smile fled from his face. "Ye *are* a brave one, lass. I'll say a prayer for ye. Now if you'll excuse me, I'll be needin' some prayers o' me own!" He turned and leaned over the rail again.

"I'll pray for you, too, Ryan Graham," Molly said.

———

Four days later, the fleet anchored at dusk. The fading sun painted the coastline orange and yellow as the longboats began their tedious chore of ferrying the gallowglass to dry land. The galleys made quicker work, as they simply ran their long prows onto the sand to allow the soldiers to disembark.

Perhaps it was the evening light, but Molly thought the gallowglass looked more menacing than they had during the voyage. They were all wearing their silver chain-mail now, and their battle axe heads gleamed as they rested the handles over their shoulders and marched onto the shore.

Toby spoke earnestly to MacDougall near the forecastle. "Just follow the shoreline south and east. Rockfleet is only about ten miles. We have to move at night, because the light would reflect off the chain-mail during the day. If we can gain surprise, we'll have the advantage."

"You'll have the advantage anyway, Master Bourke," MacDougall grunted. "The gallowglass are here."

"And I'm glad of it. We'll take the ships around to Achill Sound and slip into the bay. Hopefully we can create a distraction at the same time you're ready to attack."

"'Tis a sound plan. We canna fail."

"Any plan can fail. But this one won't, if Granuaile still holds the castle. The moon is past quarter full and waning, which will give us some darkness. May the saints go with you, MacDougall!"

Molly watched the night swallow the lines of silvery ghosts. She was amazed they could move so quietly. At last the gallowglass were gone, and the steady lapping of the tide along the shore was the only sound to be heard.

"Let's get the galleys back into the water!" Toby commanded in an undertone.

"Aye, sir," Caleb responded. He moved among the sailors, whispering orders.

"I need to see Myles. Want to tag along?" Toby asked.

"Sure!" Molly whispered with delight.

Myles was in his usual position back on the poop deck. The navigator had the best view from there, and it was close to the rudder if changes in direction were called for.

"Myles. A word!" Toby said softly. "We need to move around to Achill Sound by dawn. Can you lead the fleet through these islands safely at night?"

"I know these islands like the back o' me hand," Myles replied. "And it's a good thing, too, what with young commanders orderin' ships to sail around in the dark." He grinned, his gapped teeth gleaming in the pale moonlight.

"I knew I could count on you!" Toby slapped the old man's shoulder affectionately. "Molly, you should get some sleep. There will be lots of action come sunup, and you'll want to be rested."

"No problem. Just wake me up if Myles bumps into any islands." She winked at Myles, who responded with a quiet chuckle.

Dawn found Granuaile's fleet floating below Kildownet Castle, the watchtower overlooking Achill Sound. "We're ready," Toby breathed softly. "Signal the attack, Caleb!"

With a few energetic hand signals the galleys raced forward into Clew Bay, their oars churning the water into white foam. The *Banshee* followed close behind, her lateen sails making the most of the contrary wind. Lumbering in the *Banshee's* wake, the *Trident* gallantly tried to move her greater bulk using the single lateen sail on her mizzen-mast.

"They'll see us first from the top of Rockfleet Castle," Toby whispered. "Clare may signal as well, they can *certainly* see us." He nodded curtly at the big island off their starboard side as they passed close by.

Molly could see the masts of the tall English galleons as the Irish ships approached Rockfleet. Flashes of gunfire popped from the arrow slits in the castle walls as the defenders fired their muskets, leaving white smoke to float up into the morning sky. When the shore came into view, Molly gasped with excitement.

A tsunami of three hundred gallowglass raced along the shore toward the English force, battle axes at the ready. The English soldiers were in a clear panic, retreating to their ships as quickly as possible. The English threw away anything that burdened them; even weapons were left behind as they fled.

The Tudor ships raised their sails as they received longboat after longboat filled with frantic soldiers. The musket fire from the castle added to the overall confusion, though the shots missed most of their targets.

A pair of English warships guarding the perimeter of the fleet saw the danger of Grania's fleet sweeping in from Clew Bay. They turned broadsides to the approaching Irish ships, warning them against too much boldness.

"Hold your fire." Toby looked carefully at the assembling English fleet. "Let's not get too close. There are still twenty of them, and they have more cannon than we do. But it looks like they're licked. Let them run."

The English ships limped out of Clew Bay with far less bravado than when they'd entered. Molly watched as they struggled into the wind, turning south to Galway City and a more welcoming shore.

The *Margaret* touched the beach and Toby and Molly leaped into the surf. They slowed long enough only to pull on their shoes before sprinting to the castle.

Granuaile stood framed in the doorway, dirty but unbowed.

The children stopped, breathing hard. "Everything all right — here, Mam?" Toby gasped.

"Well enough. We were just about out o' food when ya showed up. Grand timing, Toby! Ya caught the bloody English completely off guard by landin' the gallowglass to the west. They didn't even have a chance to burn the outbuildings, ya came on them so quickly."

"The kitchen is still standing? Did they leave some food there, too?" Molly grinned.

"What's this? I see a young girl dressed like a pirate, seemin' not a bit worse for wear after more than two weeks at sea! Is this the tender young thing I left in your charge, Toby?" Granuaile's blue eyes sparkled like the water in the bay. "How was Donegal, Molly O'Malley?"

"Not quite what I expected. I'll eventually find what I'm looking for. I just don't know where I'll find it yet."

Granuaile raised an eyebrow as she glanced at her son.

"Molly's not quite what I expected, either, Mam. I'll fill you in after things settle down." Toby nodded toward the bay. "I'd best see to the ships."

"My boy is being mysterious, Molly," Granuaile murmured as Toby ran off. "We've had nothing but excitement since ya showed up."

"Oh, I'm sure that things will settle down now," Molly said. "We're a long way from Donegal." She sighed and looked across the bay. "And a long way from home."

chapter ten

Discovery

olly couldn't believe how quickly things got boring. "And I thought it was awful when Aunt Shannon didn't have television," she grumbled to herself. "Well, I solved my boredom before when I went for a walk. I'll just try not to get lost in the fog this time."

She started up the road toward Burrishoole. *I've heard that the abbey there is pretty,* she thought. Before she had gotten two hundred yards the sound of a raised voice a few feet off the path distracted her.

Molly pushed through the foliage and peeked into the clearing. It was one of the gallowglass soldiers, tall and strong, wearing his bright chain-mail made of thousands of metal rings. His back was toward her, and he seemed to be poking something with the head of his axe. "None o' your tricks, now! Don't you move an inch or I'll split you like a melon!"

The gallowglass moved slightly to his left, and Molly could now see the object of his attention.

She gasped.

The small man standing before the soldier trembled in fright, holding his floppy hat to his chest. His red hair and beard were not that unusual, and his clothes were typical for a country peasant, rough and homespun but sturdy. This was no peasant, however.

"A leprechaun," she whispered.

The leprechaun looked up at her in fear, his eyes sending a silent plea for help.

"Don't you be lookin' away from me, you sly devil, there's no one there! Now you tell me where you hide your gold, or I'll squash you flatter than a dung beetle!" The gallowglass soldier thrust his axe roughly at the red-haired elf, nearly knocking him down.

If there's one thing I've learned in the past couple of weeks, it's to use your brain instead of your brawn. This soldier could hold me off with no trouble at all. As much as I'd like to kick him ... no, think, Molly. The chain-mail ... ouch. Molly took a deep breath.

"Who are you talking to?" she called out as she pushed into the clearing. Molly put on her biggest smile and winked at the leprechaun, who let his face show relief for only an instant before bowing his two-foot tall frame in submission.

"Stop throwing your voice!" The soldier demanded.

"Are you all right, sir?" Molly stepped beside the gallowglass soldier. "I don't know anything about throwing my voice." She looked at the leprechaun, quivering a yard away from them. "What have you got there, a rabbit?"

"What in — where did *you* come from? Go away, lass, he's mine!"

"Oh, no, if you've got a rabbit in there, you've got to share. I'm tired of porridge every night." She stepped in front of the menacing axe head, and then turned to face the soldier. "Where did you say it was? I don't see anything!"

Frantically the large soldier craned his neck to look around the girl, then he shoved her to the side and began pushing the leaves aside with his axe blade. He turned on Molly in fury. "He's *gone!* The leprechaun's gone!"

"Leprechaun? What leprechaun?" Molly asked innocently, her eyes wide. "I thought you said it was a rabbit."

"No, it was you who said it was a rabbit ... you — you did that on purpose! You helped him escape!"

"Sir, I think you've been out in the sun too long. Why don't you put your helmet back on and ..."

"Nay," he growled. "I think I'll teach you a lesson. One that you won't soon forget!" He raised a mailed hand high, ready to strike.

Molly screamed and put her hands in front of her face.

"Soldier! Halt where you are!" a new voice shouted.

The gallowglass snarled and continued to step toward Molly. "And who are you, boy?"

"I am Tibbot-ne-Long Bourke, son of Richard-in-Iron, and more particularly Grania O'Malley, whose service you are currently in!"

"Why should I listen to you? You're still just a boy!"

Toby donned his enigmatic smile again. "Just a boy? Are you thinking clearly, soldier? You're saying you would rather have this discussion with Grania O'Malley?"

The soldier's face blanched, and he stuttered, "No, no o' course not ... I'm a loyal servant of her Lordship Grania O'Malley, but this girl here let my leprechaun get away and ..."

"What?" Toby's face was livid. "Are you the child here, spouting off about leprechauns as an excuse to bully a girl? And not just any girl, but a favored guest of Granuaile herself?"

"A g-guest? I didn't realize ..."

"Get out of here before I make you walk back to Tyrconnell! Take your helmet and your imagination with you! I only wish the helmet covered your face, for if I ever see you again ..." Toby kicked the conical helmet across the grass.

"A thousand pardons, Lord Bourke, I didn't ..."

"Go!"

The gallowglass scooped up his helmet and dashed away toward the road. Toby stared after him for a few seconds, and then turned to Molly.

"That was the bravest thing I ever saw," she whispered.

They stared at each other for a few seconds, and then both burst out laughing.

"You could have gotten yourself killed ..."

"You're the brave one, Molly ..."

"What if he hadn't believed you ..."

"... picking on a gallowglass three times your size ..."

"Wait." Molly caught her breath. "What were you doing, following me?"

"I'm still responsible for you. Look, I leave you alone for ten minutes, and you bewitch a perfectly sound mercenary into babbling on about leprechauns. Who knows what would happen if you had an hour to yourself!"

"But that's why I did it! Toby, I saw a leprechaun! That soldier was threatening him, trying to steal his gold! He ..."

"Shh-shh-shh. It's okay, Molly. Calm down." He gently pulled her arms to her sides.

"But ..."

"It's all right. I saw the leprechaun."

Molly's face was moist with the tears that had started. "Y-You what?"

"Little fellow, about two feet tall, red hair and beard, plain clothes, floppy hat."

She stared at him. "You *did* see him."

Toby nodded. "I believe you, Molly. I believe *everything.*"

Molly and Toby had lunch together. The mutton and porridge were surprisingly good, for the English had continued to stock the kitchen well during their siege. They decided to take their meal to a quiet spot outside away from the castle on the edge of the woods.

'So you believe me now," Molly said between mouthfuls.

"Well, the part about the leprechauns and fairies, sure enough. I'm still not ready to believe that I'm just an idea floating around in this place you call Glimmer."

"You're so stubborn!" Molly exclaimed.

He smiled. *I wish he'd stop doing that.* "I'm not the only stubborn one around here. Anyway, I don't think we should tell Mam about this. Not just yet."

"When, then?"

"Can you imagine telling Granuaile that she's a figment of someone's imagination?"

Molly gulped. "Not even in Glimmer."

"Let me think about it for a while. You may have been living in this world of fairies for a while now, but it's all new to me."

"I understand," she sighed. "Maybe I can find the leprechaun again and he can guide me to Castle Tiarnach."

"Now that makes sense. I wouldn't share it with anyone else, though."

Molly found herself drawn back to the woods where she saw the leprechaun. The spot was bare, and though she looked closely for tell-tale footprints, she could see nothing. "Maybe leprechauns don't leave footprints," she muttered. "I never asked Paddy about that."

"And what would this Paddy know about that?"

She whirled around to find the speaker, but saw only green bushes. "Who said that?"

"Answer the question first. What do ye know about the little people?"

Molly drew a sharp breath. "You're the leprechaun I saved earlier, aren't you?"

"Aye, although I don't know why ye did it, and even less why I'm talkin' to ye now. Who is Paddy?"

"He's my best friend in the world. He's a leprechaun, too. Can I see you, please? I need your help."

"My help?" The little man stepped into the clearing. "Ye did help me this mornin', that's a fact. Not that I wouldn't have figured out a way to escape on me own."

"Yep, you're a leprechaun," Molly laughed. "And you're the best thing that's happened to me since I got here! What's your name?"

"What's yours?"

"Oh, sorry, I'm Molly. Molly O'Malley."

"Eric."

"Eric? That's a nice name. It sounds familiar ..."

"Now what's this help ye be needin'?"

"Well, I'm not really *from* here. I triggered a magic spell or something with my medallion, and it brought me here to Glimmer, but it took me about 400 years into the past. I need your help to find Castle Tiarnach so the fairies can help me get back home."

The leprechaun's bushy red eyebrows shot up. "What do ye know o' Glimmer?"

"I was there. By accident, when I rescued Paddy. We finally got back with help from the Fairy Queen and some people in her kingdom."

"Wait a minute. Ye said this magic spell brought ye *here* to Glimmer. What do ye mean by that?"

Molly looked at him in surprise. "We're in Glimmer now. That's why I need to find Castle Tiarnach and King Finvarra, so he can help me get back to the real world."

The little man sat down on a hillock and pulled his floppy hat from his head. "I haven't thought about Glimmer in a long time, girl. But I know this, we're *not* in Glimmer. We're in the real world."

Molly couldn't find the words for a second. "That's impossible!"

"I'm surprised that a big 'un like you even knows the proper name for Glimmer. I came from Glimmer, and I'm sure I haven't gone back there." Eric's eyes got a faraway look in them. "Just talkin' about it is bringin' memories back. The Build-a-Leprechun store ... how could I forget that?" He chuckled. "I spent forty years there learning how to make shoes properly. There was someone ... oh, yes, I remember McGinty, the caretaker, now. What a nice leprechaun! He took such good care of us."

"McGinty!" Molly cried. "But he's ..."

"The stories he would tell us. What whoppers! Ye know he told me that I was made by a big red-haired fairy who was travelin' with a leprechaun? He never quite felt she was tellin' the whole truth, though. He even suspected she was human."

Molly sat down on a tree stump. "McGinty was the caretaker when Paddy and I were there. He told us that leprechauns have a spell cast on them that makes them forget the store when they leave, but they can remember it later if they find it again. Or maybe if someone else brings up the subject." Her eyes widened. "Omigosh! Now I remember! Eric! That's the name I gave to the leprechaun that I made by pouring a drop of whiskey on a four-leaf clover!"

"Then the story that old McGinty told me was true?" Eric looked at Molly in wonder. "He said that my pouring was unusual."

"No, wait, you could have guessed that from what I've told you so far!"

Eric winked at her. "Was your leprechaun's last name Finegan?"

Molly stared at the elf. "How do you know that?"

"McGinty told me. It's all comin' back to me, now that you've started talkin' about the store."

"Eric ... what is *your* last name?"

"Leprechauns often take their last name from their human landowner. Me name is Eric O'Malley."

Molly covered her face with her hands. "This is too freaky, but you know things that you couldn't know otherwise." She sat up, her face brightening. "Maybe you're coming from one of *my* ideas! Maybe I'm really in Glimmer after all!"

"Oh, bollocks," Eric groaned. "What will it take to convince ye that I'm tellin' ye the truth?" He began laughing. "Oh, yes, that's right, ye've known too many leprechauns to trust one!"

"I trust Paddy. Well, sort of. Sometimes it takes him a while to come around to the truth, except for that time he used the firinne spell."

Eric's eyes lit up. "He didn't!"

"He did. And after that we trusted each other."

The leprechaun stared at the ground for a moment. "Well, seeing as ye apparently made me, I suppose I should be trustin' ye as well. Maybe this will help ye trust me, too."

"What will?"

Eric grinned. "What I want to show ye. We'll need a boat. At least for you."

"What, like one of the galleys or the caravel?"

"No, no, just a wee rowboat. We need to go to one o' the small islands in Clew Bay."

Molly pursed her lips. "I'll probably need to get Toby's help for that. I have no idea where to get a rowboat, much less row one."

"Who's this Toby?"

"Did you hang around long enough to see the blond-haired boy who came up after I saved you? He told the gallowglass soldier to leave me alone."

"Ah, Toby o' the Ships? Ye've been rubbin' elbows with the upper crust, Molly! I slipped away just after the mercenary left. Can ye trust this Toby, then?"

It was Molly's turn to smile. "Toby saw you."

"Did he, now?" Eric scratched his head. "And he's all right with that?"

"I think that seeing you finally made him believe that I'm not making up all of this about leprechauns and magic and dragons ..."

Eric raised a bushy eyebrow. "We *really* must get that boat. Here's what we'll do ..."

Toby sighed as the last soldier left. "I hope everything is settled down now. Finding campsites for three hundred gallowglass is harder than I thought," he muttered to himself.

"Not everything is settled down, yet." He spun to face Molly, who had come up behind him.

He smiled and relaxed. "Not where you're concerned, anyway. What do you have there?"

Molly gently stroked the furry white head that poked out from a carrying sack slung to hold the weight in front of her. "It's my new friend. His name's Eric. Isn't he cute?"

"Where did you find a ferret? They're always half-wild, you know." Toby scratched the ferret under his chin, who closed his red eyes and began purring.

"Oh, yes, I know. This one will never be tame." Molly suppressed a snicker. "I, uh, have another favor to ask. I need to borrow a boat."

"Molly, I can't take you to Donegal right now. Maybe when we take the gallowglass back in September after the fighting season ..."

"Oh, I don't need to go to Donegal right now. Just over to one of the little islands in the bay." She smiled sweetly at him.

He looked doubtfully at her. "What's this all about?"

Molly shrugged. "You know me. Always some new thing that I can't explain and you can't believe. All I can tell you is that it's important."

"You're going to be the death of me." Toby sighed and looked down the beach. "I suppose you'll be wantin' me to take you there."

"Oh, *would* you? That would be grand!"

"Knock it off, Molly. I was helping you before because you were a mystery, and I needed to find out what you were up to. Now that I've actually seen a leprechaun, I believe you. If you want to take a stupid boat out in the bay, I'll go along with it. You don't have to twist my arm."

"Sorry. I'm just in a better mood after seeing the leprechaun. Can we go right now?"

"I suppose so. Can you tell me anything at all about where we're going? Which island, maybe?"

Molly nodded. "Once we get underway, I'll tell you everything. I promise you won't be disappointed."

They commandeered a currach, one of the small round boats that seemed to be everywhere, and pushed off into the smooth waters of Clew Bay. Toby pulled on the oars, taking them past the first island and out of sight of the shore.

"Okay, slow up for a second," Molly said. She looked down at the ferret. The ferret looked back at her, and then fixed its eyes on Toby. The red eyes melted into sparkling green, the white furry head sprouted red hair, and the albino face turned pink. Eric O'Malley smiled at Toby from his comfortable bed in Molly's carrying bag.

"It's the leprechaun!" Toby whispered. "He's really here!"

"Toby Bourke, meet Eric O'Malley. As far as we can tell, Eric is the leprechaun I made when I was in Glimmer last winter. Well, last winter for me, anyway." Molly wriggled with pleasure. "Eric says he has something interesting to show me."

"And I'm along because you needed someone to row the boat?" Toby's eyes twinkled and the corner of his mouth turned up.

"That's just a bonus. I wouldn't think of leaving you behind on something like this. Which island is it, Eric?"

The elf pointed to a nearby wooded island. "Over there. Keep your voices down, now. This could be a little dangerous."

"Now you tell me," Molly muttered.

They landed softly in a sheltered cove. Eric held his finger to his lips and led the way inland. Molly and Toby followed, trying to avoid snapping twigs as they walked.

The leprechaun stopped at the edge of a clearing and crouched down, motioning the children forward and pointing into the glen. Molly held her breath as she brushed some leaves aside to get a better look.

A large black dragon lay on the grass. Its sides moved slowly, jerking slightly with each breath. It rolled slightly, revealing a thin blue stripe that ran the length of its body.

Molly gasped and pushed into the clearing, ignoring Toby and Eric's shocked faces. She took a deep breath.

"Nefra?"

chapter eleven

A Timely Meeting

the dragon lifted her head, a deadly hiss escaping between the half-bared fangs. "How do you know that name?"

Molly stopped in her tracks and slowly raised her palms to the dragon. "You *are* Nefra, aren't you? It's all right, Nefra, no one here will hurt you."

"I said how do you know that name?!"

"Uh — you told me yourself."

Now the dragon growled and her yellow eyes glowed. Steam escaped from her nostrils. "I've never seen you before in my life. This is a trick — "

"Oh, yeah, that's right. We *haven't* met yet. Nefra, you're just going to have to trust me, like you trusted Morubek. I'm guessing that my voice is kind of echoing in your head right now."

The yellow eyes registered shock, and her mouth hung slack for a moment. "Yesss, your voice is inside my head. How do you know of Morubek, a man dead nearly three centuries?" She exhaled, and a wave of heated air blew gently over Molly, Toby, and Eric. "I am Nefra. Who are you?"

"I'm Molly O'Malley, and I'm your friend. This is Toby Bourke, and this is Eric O'Malley. Nefra, what are you doing here?"

Nefra sighed. "Two nights ago I risked a flight over the coastline. The moon was still a sliver, and it was cloudy. But the wind opened a gap in the clouds, and a soldier must have caught a glimpse of me. I fell here."

"You fell? I don't understand."

The black dragon struggled to lift her body off the ground, wincing in pain with the effort. Toby gasped as he saw the bat-like right wing hanging limp, pierced by a dark arrow. "Her wing!" he cried.

"Oh!" Molly cried as she followed Toby's gaze. "Nefra, you need help!"

"I have had no help from any man since Morubek."

"Well, you're going to get some help now. Toby, Eric, let's take a closer look. Nefra, will you let us see how badly you're hurt?"

Molly confidently stepped around Nefra's great head, sweeping her hand gently along the great jaw as she passed. Nefra started in surprise, but relaxed as Molly smiled. Toby and Eric followed more cautiously, watching the razor-sharp talons on Nefra's front legs that lay only inches from where they walked.

"Ugh. Toby, I hope you know more about arrow wounds than I do." Molly grimaced as she peered at the injury.

"It's a crossbow bolt, short but heavy." He looked at the feathers on the arrow's base. "English." He spat the word out with disgust. "It must have come from the force that was besieging Rockfleet."

"Can you get it out?" Molly asked worriedly.

"I think so. It's gone all the way through. Nefra, I'll try not to hurt you more, but this may sting a bit." Toby pulled out a sharp knife.

"What can I do?" Molly asked.

"Hold the shaft as still as possible. I'm going to cut the fletching off so we can pull the bolt straight through to the other side."

"Can't we just pull it back the way it came in?"

He shook his head. "The head is wider than the shaft. It would catch if we tried to pull it back. These crossbow bolts are heavier than regular arrows, or I'd just break the back end off and pull it through. Hold the shaft still; this won't take long."

Toby gently sliced the feathers off, trying not to wiggle the shaft as he cut. Soon the feathers lay on the ground. He looked up at Nefra. "Are you ready? It's going to hurt for a second."

"I am ready." The black dragon turned her head away. "I'm not afraid to watch," she explained. "I just wouldn't want to accidentally roast my doctors ..."

"Good thought. I did feel the heat from your breath when we first came into the clearing. Thank you." Toby looked at Molly. "Molly, why don't you pull the bolt from the back side and I'll push it from the front? We need to keep it as straight as possible."

Molly nodded. She breathed deeply and grasped the bolt firmly behind the wicked-looking triangular arrowhead. "Here goes." She pulled the bolt quickly and smoothly through Nefra's wing.

"It's out." Molly dropped the red-stained shaft to the ground. "What do we do now?"

Eric cleared his throat. "Now we clean and bandage the wound. Fetch some salt water and rinse that wing — it'll sting some more, but it usually does the trick. I know a bit about medicines and herbs. I'll look around for the right plants on the island."

Nefra sat gallantly still while Toby poured the sea-water over the ragged hole in her wing. Soon Eric returned with his work apron filled with roots, leaves, and pieces of bark. He spread them on the ground and began grinding some of the roots into a paste using a flat rock as a base.

"Let's put some o' this on the wound itself," the leprechaun said, generously spreading one of the pastes onto the injured wing. "Now, Molly, would ye hand me some o' those broad leaves there? That's the girl!"

Eric covered each leaf with a gooey mixture from another of his paste-piles and pressed them onto the wing. The elf soon had several layers of sticky leaves glued over the wound on each side of Nefra's leathery wing.

"Let that set, now. We'll have to come back and put on fresh leaves and paste every couple o' days for a while. I've seen this work before on animals. Hopefully it'll work on dragons as well." He sighed and wiped his hands clean on the grass.

"Thank you all," Nefra murmured softly.

"Oh!" Molly said, putting her hand to her cheek. "You won't be able to hunt for a while. What do you eat?"

"Hopefully not leprechauns," Eric grumbled.

"Too hard to catch," Nefra replied with a toothy grin. "I can go several weeks without food. But I have been eating fish that I catch in the ocean."

"I can get some fish for you," Toby frowned. "I'll figure out a way to sneak some from the catches that the fishermen bring in. Hopefully the fishing will be better now that the English are gone."

"I'll help, too. I'll come and visit with you until you're better again." Molly's eyes glowed with excitement.

"I would like that," Nefra purred. Her eyes blinked and started to close.

"Are you all right, Nefra?" Molly asked in alarm.

"Just tired. I'm glad to get that stick out of my wing, though." The dragon opened her mouth in a wide yawn.

"Maybe we should let you rest. Come on, Molly, Eric. We can come back tomorrow with the fish." Toby smiled thinly. "A real, live dragon. I can hardly believe it."

As the trio made their way back to the beach Molly looked back one last time. Nefra was already asleep.

Toby rowed steadily as the little currach bumped gently over the waves on the way back to Rockfleet. Eric had transformed once again into his ferret form and rested lazily in her carrying pouch.

"You'll stay with us until Nefra is better, won't you, Eric?" Molly stroked the ferret's head until he closed his red eyes.

"Unless ye think ye can learn how to make the medicine," he yawned. "So this is really the same dragon ye've met before? I just thought it a grand coincidence that ye had seen *any* dragons."

"Oh, she's the same one, all right." Molly worked her way around to scratch behind Eric's furry white ears.

"I'd best be teachin' you how to handle a currach, then, Molly. I can't guarantee that I'll be free every day to take you to the island." Toby smiled at her. "Don't look so surprised — it's not hard. Every Irish child who lives near the water learns how to row a currach. And if it's your same Nefra, you'll have to take good care of her."

"Why is that?" Molly asked, puzzled.

"Because if you don't take care of her here and now, she won't be around to meet you in 400 years."

Molly was silent for a minute. The salty breeze blew in from the west as they approached the shore. "Toby, do you mean that I could change history — again? Not just the fairy tales, but real life things, too?"

"That's exactly what I mean. I think you have to be careful what you do."

"Then you believe that I'm from the future? I could be a danger to — oh, my!" she drew a sharp breath. "Nefra was kind of secretive when we first met. She said it would be *safer* if

I wasn't around her. It's like she knew what was going to happen, and she was being careful not to ..." Molly's eyes stretched wide. "Nefra knew I was going to come back in time to meet her! She knew because it had already happened for her!"

"And we don't know how much more Nefra knew, because we don't know what more trouble you're going to get into before you can get back home."

Molly stared at Toby in disbelief. "How can I possibly get into any more trouble than I'm already in?"

He chuckled softly. "By sharing too much of what the future will be like, I would imagine. I've never been in this position before."

"I've never been in this position before, either," Eric grumbled. "Conspiring with humans, patching up dragons." He stretched his furry white neck to the side. "Could ye get that spot just to the right, Molly? A little farther ... ah, that's it."

"There's only one of us who has been in this position before." Molly stared at Toby, and even Eric opened his eyes slightly. "Oh, it's not anyone in this boat," Toby continued. "Nefra is the key. Molly, what was Nefra's mood like at the last moment before she went through the Arch to Ellesyndria?"

"She was, well, sort of peaceful and unconcerned. Like she knew everything was going to turn out all right."

"Do you think she would have been peaceful and unconcerned if she had seen anything bad happen to you in the past?"

"No, I guess not."

"Did Nefra ever mention anything about you going back in time?"

"No. But she was always mysterious and rather vague when she talked about me. It's starting to make sense now, though."

Toby sighed. "I think it would be best if the three of us don't talk about this to anyone else. Ever."

"What," Molly exclaimed, "am I just supposed to sit around and wait for everything to turn out all right?"

"I'm saying that you need to do whatever you need to do to survive, and avoid telling people in the past about time travel, or you could jeopardize your own future. Nefra didn't spill the beans in your time, and you need to be just as careful not to tell anyone in this time. That goes for all of us."

"Nefra's already in the know," Eric chimed in from his hammock. "You're going to have to tell her enough so she will repeat history for ye. It sounds like a grand story, but I don't think ye should be tellin' even me, or I could wind up bein' the one that changes everything."

"Then what exactly should I do?" Molly snapped.

"Do the right thing," the ferret whispered. "Ye don't know if your actions will cause history to repeat the way it did before, or if it will change it to be somethin' new. But it's the same for all of us, Molly. We can't act based on how we know things will turn out. All we can do is the right thing, the thing that helps make life better or safer, every time, all the time, as much as we can, as best we can. All we have is the present. Let the future take care of itself."

Molly looked down at the white ball of fur. "Are you sure you're a leprechaun?"

Eric shrugged. "McGinty said that me pourin' was unusual. There's not that many humans ever get the opportunity to build a leprechaun. I should be tryin' to get away from ye humans, but I feel ... comfortable, somehow. Like it's right to be here."

The currach bumped gently onto the shore. "Let's keep the conversation down, now, my friends," Toby whispered. "We're back in the world that's not ready for talking ferrets just yet."

chapter twelve

By Land and Sea

Molly descended the ladder from her sleeping-loft in Elva and Liam's attic two steps at a time. She hummed to herself as she hit the floor, turned around and almost crashed into Liam's rounded bulk.

"Hello there, young lady, you're in a chipper mood this mornin'," he grinned. "Up with the rooster, too, I might add."

"Oh, good morning, Liam! Sorry, I didn't see you. I guess I am in a pretty good mood. Thanks for letting me stay here; I don't know what I'd do without Elva and you."

Liam scratched his unruly beard. "It's not a bother; ye spend most o' your time with Master Toby. El is just fixin' up some eggs for breakfast; will ye join me?"

"Sure, I guess. Where'd you get the eggs?"

"From Mary O'Grady up at Burrishoole," Elva chimed in from the fireplace, where she stirred a golden liquid in a cast-iron pot. "Their chickens laid well last night, and Toby brought some o' the extra by."

"Toby? He's been here already and left without me?"

"Eat, girl. He'll be back. He had an errand to run." Elva lifted the pot from the fire and scooped the steaming scrambled eggs onto three plates. "Has a surprise for ye, he said."

"A surprise. Hmph. Just what I need." Molly shoveled some eggs into her mouth and reached for the glass of buttermilk as Elva was still pouring it.

"By Saint Patrick's mountain, El, ye were right about this girl! She eats like a horse!" Liam grinned as he attacked his own mountain of eggs.

"I can live with that, dear husband. If not for Molly and Toby bringing the gallowglass, the English would likely have burned this cottage to the ground and everything else they could put the torch to." Elva smiled at Molly, who smiled back wearing a frothy white buttermilk mustache.

"Anyone home?" Toby's voice came from the front door.

"Come on in, Toby," Elva called. "Ye know the door's always open for ye."

"That smells delicious, Elva," he sniffed as he stepped across the threshold. "No, Molly, finish your breakfast, you'll need it today."

Molly sat back down after half-rising to leave. "Uh-oh. Does this have anything to do with my surprise? It sounds like work."

"Absolutely." Toby's blue eyes twinkled above his curved smile. "You missed some buttermilk, right there …"

"I got it." Molly licked her upper lip and grinned. She returned to her eggs and finished before Liam.

"Molly, where's that animal o' yours?" Elva looked around, her eyes narrowed. "I'll not have that beast loose in me house …"

"Omigosh! He was still asleep!" Molly turned toward the loft. "Eric! Come down here, boy!"

The white ferret appeared at the top of the ladder, blinking his red eyes.

"C'mon, sleepyhead!" Molly urged, holding her pouch open wide. "Time to go!"

Eric yawned, then scampered effortlessly down the ladder and slithered into Molly's pouch, curling up immediately. "I'll get him something to eat later," Molly said as she rubbed the furry nose.

"Good day to you, Liam, Elva." Toby swung the door open for Molly.

"I know what my surprise is, anyway," Molly grinned. "You said you were going to show me how to row a currach today. When do we get to ..." she stepped outside and drew in a sharp breath.

"Oh, you ruined the surprise!" he chuckled. He led her firmly by the hand to a pair of fine-looking ponies hitched in front of the cottage. "First, though, I'll have to teach you the difference between a currach and a pony. The ponies don't take to the oars well at all."

"Oh, no, I couldn't ..." she looked at Toby, shaking her head.

"You can and you will." One of the ponies, of course, was King, Toby's own sleek black stallion. Standing quietly next to the ebony steed was a beautiful powder-grey mare. Toby gently stroked the mare's muzzle. "This is Duchess. She is strong and gentle, just the pony for you to learn to ride on."

Molly reached out to pat the grey neck and Duchess responded by rubbing her head against Molly's hand. "Duchess, you're beautiful. She's awfully big to be a pony, isn't she?"

"These are Connemara ponies. They are the largest breed to still be called ponies. Mam brought them in from County Galway when she returned to Umhall after Dónal's death. She was queen in Connemara for years, you know. The Connemara Pony is bred to handle the mountains and rough terrain there. They have good stamina, but are gentle and easy to handle. Duchess is a bit smaller than King, which should make it easier for you to climb into the saddle."

"Well, you'll have to show me everything. I don't know anything about horses — or ponies." Molly scratched the mare behind her ears.

"You should probably set Eric down while you get Duchess ready." Molly nodded and carefully slipped the pouch from her neck and shoulder, resting it against the stone wall. Eric lifted his head and blinked his red eyes.

"I brought Duchess over with just a halter on her so you could learn how to saddle and bridle her. First thing, make sure she's tied up while you're working on her." Toby touched the leather straps that wrapped around the mare's nose and head. "A halter buckles around the horse's head and has a rope you can tie up to a post or ring so she can't wander off. We'll put the bit in her mouth last; we want Duchess to be as comfortable as possible while you put the saddle on."

"Okay, she's tied up. What's next?"

"Take this brush. We need to make sure that the pony's back is perfectly smooth where the saddle will sit — no dirt, no burrs, and no hair sticking up or lying the wrong direction."

Molly brushed Duchess' coat from front to back where she thought the saddle would be. "She seems to like it," Molly said.

"She does. King likes his brushing, too. Make sure you get around the other side as well. You're doing fine."

Finally the grey coat shone in the morning light, smooth and lustrous. "Now we put the saddle on?" Molly asked.

"Not yet. You need a blanket underneath to keep the saddle from rubbing on her back. Here's the blanket; just set it where the saddle goes, you'll see how it fits. Keep the rings on the top; we'll tie those to the saddle later so it won't slide around." Toby handed her an oval shaped blanket with some metal rings sewn on the top side.

"How does that look?" Molly smoothed the wrinkles from the saddle blanket.

"Grand! You must be gentle now when putting the saddle on or the pony will be nervous the next time. Try to lift the saddle over Duchess' back and set it gently on the blanket."

Molly lifted the saddle. It was not like the saddles she saw in on Westerns on TV; this one didn't have the distinctive horn sticking up on the front and it was curved like a big Pringle's potato chip. She lifted it high over her head and strained to set it carefully on the pony's back, grunting with the effort. Her strength gave out as she swung it across the blanket and Molly had to push to keep the saddle from sliding down the mare's side.

"That's heavier than I thought!" she gasped, struggling to shove the saddle back up into place.

"You'll get the hang of it. Lift it up to adjust it again. You'll slide the blanket out of place if you push it like that."

After several more false starts, followed by circling Duchess at least three times while tugging the saddle blanket back into place, the leather saddle seemed to be in the right spot.

Toby nodded approvingly. "Now reach under her and grab that long leather strap. That's the girth. Pull it under her belly to the left side, here."

"So, this girth thing holds the saddle on?"

"Yes, it does. Buckle it here, but don't get it too tight yet. Ponies will often take a deep breath and hold it when you first tighten a girth; you have to wait for them to exhale to tighten it again to the right tension. Check the blanket again to be sure her coat is smooth underneath it, and that the saddle is lined up on top of it. We can tie these small leather strips on the saddle to the rings on the blanket. That way they'll stay together and not slide around."

Molly tied the saddle to the blanket rings and ran her hand under the blanket to check that all was smooth along Duchess' back. "Now do I tighten the girth some more?"

"Have Duchess take a step forward. That usually makes her relax. There, she breathed; tighten it now. You should be able to get your fingers comfortably under the girth belt."

"Looks good. What's next?"

"Next we put the bridle on, so you can control Duchess better when you're riding. The difference between a halter and a bridle is that a bridle has two reins instead of a rope, and it also has this metal piece called a bit that goes into the mouth."

"Isn't that painful?" Molly bit her lip.

"Only if she fights it, or if the rider yanks the reins too hard. Let me show you." Toby put his fingers into Duchess' mouth and pried it open. "See her teeth? There's a space between her front teeth and the back molars. That's where the bit goes."

"Toby, I don't want to hurt her."

"You won't. You should guide the pony mainly with your legs and knees, and use only gentle pressure from the reins to let her know where you want to go."

Molly slid the bit into Duchess' mouth and felt it slip securely between the pony's front and back teeth. Toby showed her how to hook up the bridle straps, leaving room for her fingers to slide beneath the leather. Then they took off the halter.

"We're just about ready to go. Here're the stirrups, toward the front of the saddle. Keep your feet in them so *you* won't slide off." Toby smiled.

Molly put the pouch around her neck again and tickled Eric's chin. Toby made a cradle with his hands for Molly's foot, "Up you go, now, and don't jerk on that bridle!" She stepped up and swung her right leg over the saddle.

"I'll adjust the length of these stirrup straps for you," he said as Molly found the stirrups with her feet. "Sometimes you need to take them up when you ride a lot and the leather stretches. We'll be good for today while you're learning, though." Toby raised the stirrups higher using the strap buckles. Another layer of polished leather covered the buckles to protect Molly's legs.

"Well, what do we have here?" Granuaile walked up, smiling at the two children.

"Toby's teaching me how to ride," Molly grinned. "I'm nervous, but Duchess seems gentle."

"Aye, that she is," Granuaile nodded. "Is that a new pet ye have now, Molly?"

"Yes, this is Eric. He likes to stay close."

"Be careful, ferrets can sometimes bite. What are your plans now, Molly? Ya said ya didn't find what ya were lookin' for in Donegal?"

"I've — um — got another project now that I'm working on. I'm not sure why Toby is teaching me about ponies, really."

"You'll need to know, Molly, trust me. And later today I'll be showin' you how to row a boat. You *do* want to learn how to handle a boat, don't you?" Toby grinned mischievously.

"Yes, I suppose that makes sense. There's a lot of water around here."

Granuaile laughed out loud. "Surely ya remember the O'Malley motto? 'Powerful by land and sea.' You'll need to learn about both to fit in here." Her face took on a serious look. "Do ya want to fit in here, Molly?"

Molly looked at Granuaile and then to Toby, who nodded slightly. "I've taken up so much of your hospitality already, and Elva is letting me stay there, and Toby is spending so much time ..." Molly turned to the pirate queen, who was watching her intently. "I do want to fit in, and not be a bother. I feel like I need to be here right now."

"I agree," Toby joined in. "Molly should be here right now. I think she'll be a big help in ways we can't foresee yet. She just needs a little time to adapt."

Granuaile stroked her weather-beaten chin. "Somethin' tells me I'm not getting the whole story here. I believe ya, both of ya," she hastened to add as Molly's mouth opened in protest, "and I'm glad to see ya learnin' from Toby. You'll tell me when you're ready. I know Toby, and he wouldn't keep a secret from me unless it was important." Her eyes were an impenetrable grey like the bay in the distance.

"I will, Mam," Toby said cheerily as he swung into King's saddle. "I'm trying to help Molly become more independent."

"That's good. Things haven't been 'normal' around here for a couple o' years. Independence is a grand thing that we all would do well to hold on to." Granuaile waved as the riders turned to leave.

Molly's first riding lesson went well. Duchess was a fine pony, quiet and quick to respond to Molly's directions. Toby was a good teacher, demonstrating on King so Molly could see. Soon they were walking their ponies around the grounds near the castle with no problems.

"What are in those bags?" Molly asked, noticing the canvas sacks slung in front of King's saddle.

"Fish from this morning's catch. I thought Nefra could use a bite. Besides, we should take a break from riding now. Your seat will wear out faster than the rest of you on a pony."

"You don't have to convince me of that," Molly groaned, rubbing her backside.

They tied the ponies under a shady tree near the shore, where Toby had left a small currach earlier. The three passengers pushed off into the bay, and Toby handed Molly the oars.

The small boat spun as the oars splashed first on one side and then the other. "Oh! I'm just going around in circles!" she grumbled.

"Pull on the oars at the same time!" Toby laughed. "Go slow until you get the hang of it. That's it, now try going straight for a while. When you need to change direction, just pull a little softer on the side you want to turn toward for a couple of strokes. Then go back to rowing straight again. Don't make any sudden changes."

Eric crawled out of his carrying-pouch and transformed into his usual leprechaun form. "I don't mind the fur so much, but this craving I get for red meat when I'm a playin' a ferret is drivin' me crazy!"

"I have some cheese in my bag, if you'd like that." Toby opened the sack and offered the golden round cheese to the elf. Eric grabbed it and hungrily stuffed a chunk into his mouth along with a couple more into his pockets.

"Toby," Molly said, "I've been thinking about how much things have changed. I don't think it's a coincidence that I've met Nefra."

"That's true," he agreed. "You seem to attract magical and mythical creatures." He winked at Eric.

She splashed some water on Toby with an oar and made a face at him. "I'm serious! Just think of the possibilities now — or at least as soon as Nefra's wing heals. You can see stuff from the air that you might miss from the ground."

"And ye can see stuff flyin' about *in* the air that ye wouldn't see hidden behind trees," Eric added. "If ye have Nefra start flyin' all over Donegal, ye could be puttin' *her* in danger."

"We could travel at night. Nefra can see well enough in the dark for both of us. Toby, what do you think?"

He sighed. "All these fairies and leprechauns have to come from somewhere. I still agree with Eric, though, you're not in this Glimmer place you keep talking about. You're in the real world. There may not be a castle to find."

"Are you going to try to stop me?"

Toby looked into her blazing green eyes. "Molly O'Malley, I don't think there is *anyone* who could stop you." He smiled and leaned back in the boat.

Molly decided to drop the subject for now and concentrate on her rowing. She found that she could control the currach with practice. At first she turned around frequently to check her heading, but soon discovered that fixing her sights on the shore behind them seemed to work best to keep going in a straight line.

She was pleased that she remembered which island they needed to go to. The trip was slower than when Toby rowed them the first time, but she felt a deep sense of satisfaction when the little boat bumped onto the rocky shore.

Nefra was expecting them. "The wind today blows from the shore where you landed. I could smell you coming easily. Is that fish?"

"A pair of cod," Toby smiled, pulling the grey-green fish from the large bags. "Caught just this morning."

The black dragon lowered her head and bit into one of the cod. She lifted her head high and swallowed it in a single gulp. Her tongue flicked across her mouth, and her shoulders relaxed. "Thank you. I haven't eaten in several days."

"How is your wing, Nefra?" Molly asked.

"Much better, thank you. It's a little stiff, but that doesn't compare to having an arrow sticking through it."

"Well, I'd best be makin' up some more pastes to change the bandages," Eric said. "Molly, will ye help me by gatherin' some leaves as ye did before?"

"Of course." She followed the leprechaun into the surrounding woods to look for their supplies.

"You are all so kind to me. I have not felt such concern since Morubek." Nefra looked toward the departing O'Malleys.

Toby smiled. "We are all your friends, Nefra. And your wing will heal — in time."

chapter thirteen

Summonings

"Nefra," Molly said, snuggling back against the great black dragon's shoulder, "I'm so glad I found you again. I had so little time with you before."

The great yellow eyes were curious. "Does this have anything to do with what you said about meeting me before?"

"Yes. I've been coming here to visit you for over a month now. My arms are so strong from rowing that stupid currach and lifting Duchess' saddle every day I could probably pick you up myself. Toby is off practicing archery today, so he's not here to keep me from saying this, and I'm about ready to bust!"

"Molly …" Eric warned.

"Shush. Let's suppose you're right, Eric, that we're not sitting inside Glimmer and I really have traveled back in time. That's all the more reason to tell her." She turned to the dragon. "Nefra, I'm not from here. Some kind of magic brought me four hundred years into the past. My past. I met you about a year ago, according to my time. That's still way in the future for you. Do you understand what I'm saying?"

"You have strong magic, Molly O'Malley. I hear your voice inside my head when you speak. I believe you."

"Well, that's just a side-effect of ..." Molly stopped herself with an effort. "I'll explain that later. The important thing is that when we met in the future, you were a little bit ... secretive."

"Secretive?"

"Yes, like it might be *safer* if I wasn't around you for a while. At first I thought maybe you were feeling you might lose control and hurt me or something. I asked if you were dangerous, and you said 'not in the way you think.' But I think I understand now."

"What do ye mean, Molly?" Eric pressed.

"Nefra, you *knew* things. You knew I was going to come back in time, because you had already met me. And you wanted to keep that secret from me."

"Why would I do that, Molly?" Nefra's breath stung gently with sulfur.

"Because I told you to keep it secret." Molly exhaled with relief. "If you had told me I would travel back in time, I might do something to avoid doing whatever caused it to happen. A change like that could alter history."

"Since we're all out in the open about this now, didn't Toby warn ye about sharing too much about the future?" Eric snapped.

"I seem to remember a leprechaun telling me to just do whatever seemed right and not worry about the consequences! Well, this seems right to me!" Molly retorted. "And it matches what actually happened. Someone had to clue Nefra into not revealing all of this, and it might as well be me!"

"Molly," Nefra said softly. "How will you get back to your own time?"

The red-haired girl turned to the great black head, her green eyes brimming with emotion. "I don't know, Nefra. I really don't know. I'm going to try to find Castle Tiarnach and the fairies in the fall when we take the gallowglass back, but I'm not sure I'll be able to locate it. I failed before, but we were rushing to get back here to help Grania and we didn't have much time."

The dragon was silent for a moment. She lifted her right wing. "I am nearly healed, thanks to you and your friends. I am forever in your debt." Nefra lowered her head to Molly's level. "If there is anything I can do for you, name it and I will do all in my power to serve you."

"Nefra, you don't need to …"

"Yes, I do. You have but to call on me and I will be there."

"Ahem." Eric coughed, and the two girls turned to look at him. "That's all grand when you're both here, but what's to be done when Molly is on shore and you're on this island or gone to some other hideaway?"

They stared blankly at the leprechaun. "All right, I'll put it plainly, then. Ye need some way to summon the dragon, some way to call even when you're apart. Nefra's not goin' to transform into a cuddly ferret and ride around in your pouch all day."

"He's right," Molly whispered. "That is, if you really want to do this, Nefra …"

"I do."

"Well, then," Eric smiled, rubbing his hands together, "I can cast a summoning spell that should be good to let Nefra know, oh, about three times that Molly needs her. Using magic has a bonus; Nefra will feel the summons in time to actually travel from wherever she is to reach Molly's location just as Molly calls for her. It'll be like using the summons and the dragon will appear."

"This is powerful magic, small one. What is needed?" Nefra seemed somewhat amused.

"We'll need your willingness to submit to the spell, which ye've already given. Then we'll need some sort of object to hold the summoning spell; something small …" Eric looked around.

"Wait, Eric. I know just the thing." Molly pulled out her silver heart-shaped locket. She carefully opened it to reveal two pictures; her father on the left and her mother on the right. Also lying inside the case was a perfect shamrock. Molly picked up the shamrock and handed it to the leprechaun.

"What's this, now?"

"That's the same shamrock that Paddy used when he granted me three wishes."

Eric's eyes widened. "Faith, girl, ye couldn't pick a more suitable container. This looks like it was plucked but yesterday."

"More like a year ago yesterday. Is that all you need?"

He nodded. "Nefra, put your claw here, talons up. I'll lay the shamrock in the middle of it, and Molly, put your hand over the shamrock. I'll put me hands over yours. That's grand. Give me a moment to gather me thoughts."

Eric closed his eyes for several seconds, and then opened them. "I bind these two with friendship, human and dragon, flesh and scale, small and large. As these two have shown love for one another, now let this bond be made, that three times Molly O'Malley may summon Nefra, mistress of fire and flight, and may each summons bridge time and space to allow Nefra to arrive even at the moment of Molly's summoning. Both Nefra and I owe our lives to this *colleen;* I grant these summonses to her benefit. I, Eric O'Malley, declare this by the power within me."

The pile of hands and talons glowed with a faint blue light that Molly remembered from a night long ago in the Burren, when fairies danced in a circle about her and the wishes were placed in this same shamrock. The glow faded and disappeared.

"How will I make a summons?" Molly asked.

"Ye hold the shamrock, and say:

"Out of time, out of myth,
I summon you now here forthwith.
Nefra, heir of the dragon race,
come now to this time and place."

"Did you have to make it rhyme? Oh, well, it'll probably make it easier to remember." Molly placed the shamrock — which looked even greener now than it did before — back into the locket and snapped it closed. "I hope I never need to use this. Nefra, as soon as your wing is completely healed, you're going to fly me up to Donegal. We'll search for Castle Tiarnach from the air. You can't hide a castle."

"Ah, Molly me dear," Eric sighed. "Ye can hide a castle if you're lookin' for it in the real world and the castle is in Glimmer."

"Well, then, I'll know for sure, won't I?" Molly tried to smile, but her heart sank at Eric's words.

Nicholas Malby read the parchment on the desk before him, pulling the candle closer for light in the deepening twilight. He grunted as a man with a neatly-trimmed beard and a fierce-looking cutlass slung at his side entered the room.

Malby's eyes glinted with impatience as he observed his visitor. "Martin! Sit down, sit down, we have much to discuss."

Martin swept off his leather hat, weathered by sea-salt. "Governor Malby."

"*President* Malby now, Captain. Lord President of Connaught. I received the title whilst in London last fall. Now I return to find the countryside in rebellion, your attack with twenty ships — *twenty,* mind you! — your attack on the pirate woman O'Malley driven off in disgrace!"

"We will succeed next time, m'lord. Grace O'Malley is strong, but she ..."

"Will hand your arse to you on a platter! No, Martin, we need a far better plan to deal with this — unusual Irish woman." Malby slouched back in his chair, stroking his own beard thoughtfully. "What is her strength, Captain?"

"Her navy, sir. No one knows the broken Irish coastline like Grace O'Malley. Her galleys row out and rob the slower merchantmen, and then she sails back to disappear into the inlets and island-mazes along the coast. Our galleons cannot find her. And she is the devil incarnate when attacked in her castle. Powerful by land and by sea, that's her family motto."

Malby leaned forward to whisper, making the candle-flame flicker. "Then we shall rip her strength from her. Grace O'Malley's not faced her devil yet. Here is my plan ..."

chapter fourteen

Kidnapped

Molly awoke enveloped by the darkness. She lay quietly staring up at the thatched ceiling, waiting for her eyes to adjust. "Darn it," she grumbled under her breath. "That was a good dream, too."

She rolled over and felt gingerly along the floor until her fingers found a smooth porcelain jar with matching lid that was cool to the touch. She drummed her fingertips lightly on the lid for a second, and then she sat up.

"I've been here almost three months, and I still hate these chamber pots!" she hissed softly. Tossing her blanket from her she began pulling on her capris. "Every time you use one at night, you have to dump it in the morning — but I have to carry mine down a ladder! I'd rather make the trip to the outhouse!"

She slipped on her shoes and crept quietly down the ladder to the main floor. Elva and Liam slept in the corner bed. Liam snored loudly enough to mask any small noises Molly might make. *Good, let them sleep.*

Carefully she lifted the door latch and slipped out into the night. It was cool, and the breeze from Clew Bay was crisp and biting as it often was. Molly had never seen as many cold, cloudy days as she had experienced since arriving at Rockfleet Castle.

The outhouse was located away from the other buildings for obvious reasons, but not so far as to discourage visitors entirely. The left side of the moon glowed with silver light, heralding the morning that would soon come.

As she approached the small wooden shack, another shape appeared from the shadows. Molly froze, and whispered, "Who's there?"

The figure stopped and peered at her. "Molly, is that you?"

Molly sighed with relief. "Deirdre! What in the world are you doing out here this time of night?"

"Probably the same thing as you," Deirdre chuckled, pushing her hood back to let her flowing blond hair shimmer in the moonlight. "Little Seamus wakes easily. I didn't want to take the chance o' disturbin' his sleep. They don't call chamber pots 'thunder mugs' for nothin', ye know."

"He's getting too big to be called 'Little Seamus', isn't he? He's almost four." Molly giggled.

"Yes, and I'm grateful to ye for comin' over to play with the lad. He loves your company, and so does Myles."

"I think Myles likes to see his grandson happy. Does he know you sneaked out? Niall is still out on the fishing expedition, isn't he?"

"Mm hmm. Myles decided to help out until Niall gets back in a few days. Not that he minds spending more time with Seamus."

"Toby introduced me to Myles the first day we met. He tells such exciting stories! Can we walk this way while we talk?"

"Definitely. You go ahead first. We can walk back together."

A few minutes later the ladies strolled back through the early morning darkness, much more relaxed after visiting the outhouse. "Molly, you'll come over and see us this morning, won't ye?"

"Sure I will. I wouldn't miss ... what's that?"

They strained to hear the noise drifting through the night. A sound of a man's voice raised in alarm, then suddenly silenced. Muffled thumping sounds echoed dimly across the grass.

"That's coming from the direction of our house!" Deirdre broke into a run as Molly followed closely. The house seemed eerily dark and quiet as they approached the back door. Trembling, Deirdre opened it and choked back a cry as they stepped inside. Tables and chairs were strewn about the room and the mattress lay overturned on the floor.

"Myles? Seamus?" Deirdre cried out in terror. "Where are you?"

Molly pushed her way past the table and opened the front door. She heard what sounded like horses galloping away in the distance. A lone figure wrapped in a dark robe spun toward her as she came out of the house. His face caught the moonlight as he turned, and she saw his features clearly for a moment: a hooked nose, thin mouth and close-set eyes. His eyes narrowed to slits as he looked directly at her. He looked familiar, as if she had seen him before. Quickly he yanked his hood over his face and melted into the shadows.

"Wait! Come back!" Molly cried, but he was gone.

A wail of grief exploded from the house. Molly whirled and went back in to find Deirdre on her knees hugging Seamus' empty mattress. "He's gone! Me boy is gone!"

Molly hugged the woman's heaving shoulders for a second. "I'm going to get help," she whispered. Then she sprinted for Elva's cottage.

She slammed the door open without pausing to knock. "Elva! Liam! Something terrible has happened!"

Elva sat up in bed, groggy with sleep. "Molly? What is it, dear?"

"Someone has broken into Niall and Deirdre's house, and they've taken both Myles and little Seamus!"

"Are ye sure, girl?"

"Deirdre was with me! Oh, someone's got to get back there, she's frantic! We have to go after them, find them! I heard horses!"

Soon most of the village was milling about in nightshirts and gowns, waving lanterns and torches. Granuaile appeared, hastily dressed. "We can't see anything in the dark. We'll have to wait until the mornin'. Where's the guard? If he's sleeping ..."

Unfortunately the guard was soon discovered at his post with his throat slit. "These people are dangerous," Granuaile muttered. "Double the guard. We'll have to look at this come daylight. Someone see to Deirdre, she can't go back home tonight."

Molly pushed closer to the pirate queen. "Grania?"

"Yes, child?"

"I — I saw a man standing outside Niall and Deirdre's house right after we discovered that Seamus and Myles were missing."

"Who was it?"

"I don't know. I didn't recognize him. He looked a little familiar, though."

"Keep a sharp lookout, Molly. He may be the key to tracking down these kidnappers."

"Grania, will they be all right?"

The older woman bowed her head, shaking her salt-and-pepper hair slightly. "I can't say, dear. Sometimes rivals will take hostages to get something they want. Obviously whoever did this could have killed them tonight as they did the guard, but they didn't."

Molly couldn't get back to sleep, not that she was really trying. The sun lifted above the horizon, painting warm golden colors as it streamed through the little window in her loft. The darkness fled in the morning light, but pieces of darkness still clung to Molly's thoughts as she pondered this new mystery. Who could have taken Myles and his grandson, and why?

"Ye look like a girl with somethin' on her mind," Eric yawned from inside the pouch.

"Shh. They might hear you."

"Then let's get out o' here so ye can tell me safely. If ye'd remember to take me along during these nighttime treks o' yours ..."

"To the bathroom? Get a grip, leprechaun. C'mon, let's go."

———

Toby was at the door just after breakfast. "Molly! I heard you were there with Deirdre. Are you all right?"

"Yes, but let's go outside. I have an errand to run."

"An errand — oh, right, an errand!" His eyes brightened as he took Molly's hint.

As soon as they were safely outside, Toby started peppering Molly with questions. "Did you hear the commotion this morning, all those search parties riding off in every direction? With no rain the past couple of weeks, the ground isn't soft enough to leave decent tracks. Were you scared? Someone said you heard horses riding away. Couldn't you tell which way they went?"

"I think they went north," she sighed. "But you have to ride north first anyway, away from the bay. Then you can turn and go any direction, so it doesn't make any difference."

As they passed a nearby cottage, Molly glimpsed a man's hawk like nose and felt his close-set eyes staring at her. She turned to make sure, but the man had disappeared.

"What is it, Molly?" Toby asked.

"I thought I saw the man who was there last night. He was looking right at me from behind that corner, but now he's gone."

"Are you sure? That guy would be long gone by now."

"Toby, I know what I saw. I just don't know where he went."

"Well, if I helped kidnap someone, I sure wouldn't stick around! It's probably nothing."

They walked toward the shore and their waiting currach. "I have to fill Eric in about last night, too," Molly whispered.

"I can't believe they took Myles!" Toby shook his head. "And Seamus, too!"

Molly turned the currach over while Toby set the oars into the boat. "I managed to swipe three good-sized salmon this morning for Nefra. That may be it until the men return from the fishing trip," Toby whispered.

"Deirdre said that Niall would be back in a couple of days," Molly replied. "Oh, he's going to be heart-broken!'

Toby pushed the little boat out into the water. Molly and Toby reached for the oars at the same time. "I've got it," Molly smiled. "You're away at your lessons so often, I'm used to rowing. Everyone assumes I'm spending all day with you, and I don't discourage them. It gives me a good alibi to take the currach over and spend time with Nefra."

Toby grinned and sat back in the little boat, locking his fingers behind his blond head. "Fine by me. I'm used to Mam doing things by herself, too."

"No one would accuse Grania O'Malley of not being independent," Molly agreed. "Grania is so cool."

"Cool? Why would she be cold?"

"Um — forget I said that. I guess the Irish equivalent would be *grand.*"

Eric transformed to his normal leprechaun form. "Now tell me about last night. Somethin' queer is going on, it sounds like."

Molly filled Eric and Toby in about the noises she heard the night before, the sound of horses riding away, and the strange man she saw in the moonlight. And she was quite sure the same man was looking at her this morning. They continued talking after they landed and began walking to Nefra's clearing in the woods.

"I still think you may be having nightmares from last night," Toby said. "You were so close to the kidnapping — it's enough to make anyone imagine things!"

"I'm not imaging things, Toby! Geez, first leprechauns and dragons, now kidnappers! Are you ever going to believe me without seeing it with your own eyes?"

"He didn't believe in leprechauns?" Eric gasped. He clutched dramatically at his chest and tumbled to the soft turf.

Molly and Toby stared at the leprechaun's still form.

"Do you think I killed him?" Toby whispered.

"It's possible," she whispered back. "You have to be careful what you say around leprechauns. They're so sensitive."

"We should probably let him rest quietly. Respect for the dead and all that," he nodded.

"And why would ye walk away to leave a dead leprechaun without a proper wake?" Eric shouted, his eyes still squeezed tight. "That's worse than not believin' in the first place!"

"Eric, my friend, you are absolutely right," Toby chuckled as he extended his hand. "Let me help you up. I apologize for not believing in leprechauns."

"Apology accepted. Now let's not waste any more time squabbling between ourselves. We have a dragon to feed."

Nefra was glad to see them, and thankful for the salmon as well. "I'm happy you could come today," Nefra purred. "What were you talking about back there? That was quite a commotion."

"Oh, it's terrible," Toby answered grimly. "Myles and his grandson Seamus were kidnapped last night. Molly saw a man she believes may have been involved. And I apologize to you, Molly, for not believing you. I need to have more faith."

Molly smiled and made a delicate curtsy. "It's awful when you lose someone close. Myles is almost like family." The red-haired girl sighed. "Little Seamus is so cute. We *have* to get them back."

"Myles *is* close to me. He's an O'Flaherty," Toby said. "He came from Connemara to Umhall after Mam's first husband Dónal died. The clan wouldn't give Mam her proper inheritance, so she took three war galleys and two hundred O'Flaherty men back with her. They would rather follow Granuaile than their own clansmen!"

"That's right!" Molly exclaimed. "You're related to the O'Flahertys! So Myles is family, then?"

"Only by marriage. Mam had three children with Dónal, so I have two half-brothers and a half-sister who are O'Flahertys. Owen, the eldest, still lives in the family castle at Bunowen. He's one of the kindest people I've ever met."

"I know that castle," Nefra said. They turned to look at her. "It's on the coast near the big ocean, in the place you call Connemara. I've swum and flown by there many times."

"That's right," Toby nodded. "We usually travel there by ship. Both the O'Malleys and the O'Flahertys are sea-going clans."

"Speaking of flying, Nefra, when will your wing be healed?" Molly asked.

"I think in three or four days. It's feeling much better."

"Good." Molly exhaled. "I can't wait to go back to Donegal and search for Castle Tiarnach. I have one more reason now. The fairies might help me find Myles and little Seamus."

"I wish you the best, Molly," Toby said. "You've opened my eyes to so many things I never dreamed even existed."

"I just hope that castle exists," Molly said quietly. "If I am in the real world, I may be in real trouble."

―――――――――

"Molly! Liam and I are going for our walk now!" Elva called up into the loft.

"That's grand, El!" Molly responded. "I'm just getting ready for bed. Make sure you love-birds don't stay out too late!"

"Do ye hear the cheek from that girl, Liam? And only twelve years old!"

"She'll be as feisty as you by the time she grows up, El! Come on, let the girl get some sleep!" The couple was still chuckling as they went out the door, their voices fading quickly in the night air as they walked.

"I hope I'm that happy when I get married some day," Molly sighed. "I'm glad they can still find something they can laugh at with all of this kidnapping business."

"How do ye know you're goin' to be married?" Eric yawned. He always remained in his white ferret form while inside the house.

"Well, I don't know," she replied, "but I've got to hope. I've got to hope that I can get back home, and grow up, get married, have a family ..." She sighed. "You have to hold on to your dreams."

The cottage door below opened quietly, betrayed only by a subtle squeak of the iron hinges. "El? Liam? Did you forget something?" Molly called down.

She heard footsteps crossing the floor below, and then the ladder shook slightly from the weight of someone climbing up. "El?" Molly called again.

It was not Elva's greying hair that pushed up into the loft. Molly gasped as the now familiar close-set eyes and hawk like nose appeared above the ladder. The thin mouth curved in a wicked smile.

"Who are you?" Molly cried. "You shouldn't be here! Get out!"

"Now, now, Molly O'Malley, there's no need to raise your voice. If ye do, I'll slice ye up like the fish I gut every day before ye can get a scream out." He displayed a long knife in his right hand, the sharp edge gleaming in the dim light.

"What — what do you want?"

"Oh, just to talk a bit. See what ye know."

She shook her head vigorously, making her red hair bounce. "I don't know anything. I don't even know who you are!"

"Ah, but ye saw me last night, didn't ye, girl?" He chuckled softly. "I thought ye might have seen me then, but I knew for sure when ye tried to get a better look at me this morning. That makes ye a loose end."

Molly's mind raced. *I've got to keep him talking. I've got to learn more. And above all, I have to keep hoping there is some way out of this.*

"How could I be a loose end? I don't even know your name."

"Well, I don't see the harm in tellin' ye that. Me name's Richard O'Kelly, or so people think."

Molly frowned. "That's not your *real* name, then?"

He chuckled again. "A sharp girl, too! No, I'm not an O'Kelly. I'm from the clan Joyce."

"The Joyces!" Molly gasped. "That was the clan that killed Grania's first husband, and then she defended Hen's Castle against them."

"That castle was in our possession for years before that swaggering O'Flaherty stole it from us!"

Molly's eyes popped wide open. "O'Flaherty? The Joyces hate the O'Flahertys! And Myles is an O'Flaherty! Is that why you kidnapped him?"

Richard grinned. "That was a fortunate bonus, but quite accidental. Myles O'Flaherty is only the tool we'll use to attack Grace O'Malley herself. His grandson, o' course, is insurance so that Myles will do as he's told."

"You'll be defeated if you try to attack Grania, just like the English were beaten last March!"

"Oh ho, ye think the English are done with Grace O'Malley, then?" Molly paled and he continued. "Grace is a gambler, always has been. When she finds that we've taken her prize navigator to Castle Hackett, she'll come after him. She'll know the stakes are too high not to come. And the English will be waiting for her."

"It's a trap," Molly whispered. "You took Myles because he knows things. He knows ..." she looked up in pain. "He knows where the islands are, where the channels flow ..."

Richard Joyce tapped his temple with the flat of his blade. "He knows," he said. "Grace will have to come after him. And now *you* know too much, my little bug. No one will find your body until morning, when I will be gone from here at last. Time to say goodnight, Molly."

He stepped up one more rung on the ladder, an evil smirk on his thin lips. He held the knife out toward Molly, who backed away as far as she could. Richard climbed one more step and prepared to plunge the blade into her heart.

A white blur launched itself from a pile of cloth in the corner, and the red-eyed ferret fastened his razor-sharp teeth into the spy's arm. Richard roared in pain and rage, pulling back slightly as he flung the furry attacker away. He looked back at Molly, who had picked up a good-sized chamber pot.

"Time to say goodnight, Richard," she said, and threw the chamber pot at his head with all her might.

It struck him square on the forehead, shattering into a dozen shards. He lost his grip on the ladder and fell backwards, a cry of surprise on his lips. There was a heavy thud from below, and all was quiet.

Trembling, Molly crawled to the edge of the loft and looked down. Richard Joyce lay sprawled at the bottom of the ladder, his head and neck lying at an unnatural angle.

Eric moved to her side, and she scratched his furry head gently. "Jeepers," she said. "I'm going to be more careful going down that ladder from now on."

chapter fifteen

The Best-Laid Plans

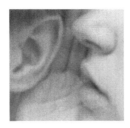

*Y*ep, he's dead, all right." Liam nudged the body with his boot.

"Molly, tell me what happened," Elva whispered as she draped a shawl around the girl's shoulders. "Here, dry those tears."

"Th-Thank you." Molly took the handkerchief Elva offered and wiped the wet streaks from her face. "Is he really dead?"

"Broke his neck when he fell off the ladder, looks like. What was he doing?" Liam scratched his scruffy beard as he peered up into the loft.

Molly took a deep breath. "I had gone to bed, just after you left. He came in and ... and he climbed up the ladder." She buried her face in the hanky.

"What did he want?" Elva asked gently. "There's nothing o' value in this cottage except for ..." Her eyes widened as she looked at Molly. "Except for you, child."

Molly looked up from the handkerchief, staring directly into the older woman's eyes. "Oh, Elva, I was so scared!" Then she covered her face again.

"Oh, ye poor thing! Did he harm ye, dear?" Elva cradled the girl in her arms.

"N-No. When he tried to attack me, Eric bit him, and I beaned him with the chamber pot. He fell backwards off the ladder. Oh, is he really dead?"

"Dead and good riddance, attacking helpless girls like that," Liam growled. "Or maybe not so helpless. Hmmm ... he looks familiar."

"He said his name was Richard something. O'Kelly, I think," Molly whispered.

"O'Kelly, that's right. I remember the dog now. Joined us a few months back," Liam nodded.

"Where's that sailor I sent to get help?" Elva growled. "He's had time to go to Burrishoole and back."

Footsteps outside announced a visitor. The door swung open and Granuaile strode in. "Is the child all right?" she demanded. "I was told ..."

Molly launched herself across the room and hugged the tall queen tightly. "Oh, Grania!" she cried.

Granuaile wrapped her arms around the girl. She looked over Molly's shoulder to Elva, her eyes questioning.

"She was attacked by this animal. He came in right after he saw Liam and me go out." Elva nodded toward Richard's body with disgust.

"I see." Granuaile nodded. "Looks like there was a fight? All these pottery fragments scattered about."

"The girl fought him off, she did," Liam said proudly. "Her ferret bit him, and she cracked his skull with the chamber pot."

"That's my O'Malley," Granuaile whispered fiercely. "We'll find a bed for ya in the castle tonight, Molly. Liam, fetch her things, please. And be careful on the ladder." She winked at the big man.

The cock crowed, but Molly was already up. She rushed out the door of Rockfleet Castle and stared down the lane. A few minutes later, a black pony galloped into view. "Toby," she sighed with relief.

He dismounted almost before King stopped and ran to her. He grabbed her shoulders. "Are you all right? I'm sorry, I'll never — "

She threw her arms around him, pressing her lips to his ear. "Shut up, you big oaf, and pretend you're consoling me. Say *nothing* about the man I saw yesterday, do you understand? Lives depend on it!"

He looked surprised for a moment, and then returned the embrace, awkwardly. "It's all right, Molly," he said stiffly.

"Tell you what, pretend we're good friends instead of actors, okay?" she said, her voice dripping honey. "I've got to look distraught, and you're almost making me laugh. I'll explain everything when we're alone."

Toby's face twitched as he controlled his own urge to smile, and he leaned his face into her hair. "If you say so, my dear friend. How soon can we be alone?"

"As soon as we saddle Duchess and go for a ride. We'll say it will help me relax after last night if anyone asks. Hurry."

As they entered the clearing, they allowed their ponies to slow to a walk. Molly twisted in her saddle, scanning in every direction.

"Ouch! A bit less of a turn, there, Molly! Ye've passengers aboard!" Eric growled from his pouch.

"Oh, I'm sorry, Eric, I'm just checking to be sure no one is around."

"Well, check here first. Can we tell the lad now?"

"Tell the lad what?" Toby grumbled. "What is going on?"

"The man I saw yesterday is the same man I saw at Niall and Dierdre's house. He sneaked into the cottage to kill me, to tie up some loose ends, he said."

"I heard you fought him off, that he was trying to ..."

"Elva assumed the worst, and I didn't exactly discourage her. That man was only there to kill me. He's one of the kidnappers; he helped plan it. I couldn't even cry after he died. I had to drip water from the wash basin down my face to make it look as though he upset me. Oh, look, *now* I'm crying, just thinking about little Seamus!"

"Then for goodness sake, Molly, we've got to tell everyone! Mam and the others need to know the truth, so we can rescue them! Let's go back and ..."

"No!" Molly hissed, wiping her eyes. "That's exactly what we can't do! It's a trap, Toby! The English are involved, and they *want* Grania to come after Myles so they can ambush her! We cannot let your mom know about this!"

"I don't understand," he said. "Why would Richard O'Kelly betray Grania?"

"Because he's not an O'Kelly. He's a Joyce."

Toby's eyes widened. "No! You're sure?"

"Told me himself, just before he tried to gut me. He also told me where they were taking Myles and Seamus, and why. Myles knows the coastline. The English want that information so Grania won't be able to escape their fleet any more. So we *can't* tell your mom or anyone else, or we'll be playing right into their hands!"

"Molly's telling ye true, she is," Eric nodded. "I heard every word o' the traitorous scum meself."

"Toby, where is Castle Hackett?" Molly frowned as she pushed a wisp of hair back from her eyes.

"Oh, it's just southwest of Tuam and a bit north from Galway City, probably two or three day's ride from here."

"Perfect." Molly nodded, doing math in her head.

"Wait," Toby said, "Castle Hackett — is that where the English are keeping them? Are you sure we shouldn't tell Mam?"

"Absolutely. We must keep this secret to protect her."

"But — but we can't just leave them there! The English can be brutal! Mam just got back from several months imprisonment in Dublin, and she almost died! They'll not stop at threatening Seamus to force Myles to reveal everything he knows!"

"I know, I know. Dear Richard implied exactly that. So there's only one thing to do."

Toby stared at Molly. "And what is that?"

Molly smiled — mysteriously, and to Toby's mind, somewhat wickedly. "You need to teach me some Irish."

chapter sixteen

Into the Net

*t*he ponies picked their way slowly along the dark road which ran across a narrow bridge of land. Molly could make out lakes far off to her left and her right. The water reflected the milky light from what was left of the moon. It was a good place to be if you wanted to hide.

"So how long do you think it will be before they notice we're gone?" she asked.

Toby rocked smoothly in King's saddle as the black pony side-stepped a hole. "A couple of days, maybe more," he yawned. "You told Mam that you wanted to spend a few days at Burrishoole to get away from Rockfleet, and I told MacTibbot that I was going to Rockfleet for a few days to help you get over your scare. By the time either of them gets the time to actually go to the other castle and check out the stories ..." he shrugged.

"And when you picked me up Sunday evening to come to Burrishoole, we skirted the castle and kept on riding. Brilliant!"

"We'll see how brilliant this all turns out in the end. This is dangerous work, Molly."

"You live in a dangerous world. I'm just trying to fit in until I can figure out how to get home."

The land broadened as they left the narrow section behind. Toby brought them toward their right, away from the road. "This is Lough Mask," he said as they pulled up by the shore. "We want to stay off the road — the town of Ballinrobe is just a couple of miles east from here. It's one of the more prosperous towns in County Mayo."

"That's a huge lake," Molly whispered as she dismounted. "I mean, it's nothing like Lake Michigan, but it's really big."

"It's half the size of Lough Corrib. Corrib is just ahead of us, and will be on our right half the night tomorrow before we turn toward Castle Hackett. Bring Duchess into this thicket. It'll be daylight soon, and we need to find cover."

Eric grunted as Molly dropped her pouch gently to the ground. "Wakey, wakey," she hummed.

"Camping already?" he yawned. "Time for this leprechaun to wake up." The snow-white ferret transformed into the red-haired leprechaun. He stretched and scratched his head.

"You know the drill," Molly grinned. "Toby and I ride at night while you sleep. Then you stand guard during the day while we sleep."

"Fine with me. I need the time when I can be a leprechaun again. Sometimes I wonder if I'm a fairy or a ferret."

Molly smiled warmly at him. "You do make an adorable ferret, but you make a better leprechaun. And I'm not saying that just because I helped make you. You were so brave, biting Richard Joyce's arm when he was ready to stab me. You saved my life!"

"Aye, I did, didn't I?" Eric winked at Molly and stretched out under a spruce tree. "I'll just make meself comfortable until ye fall asleep."

"You'd be more useful if you'd cast some camouflage spells around this thicket," Toby chuckled. "Something to help actually *hide* the ponies while they're standing behind the trees? They usually sleep standing up, you know."

"Never fear, Master Toby! I shall disguise the ponies, secret a handsome Gaelic prince, and cloak our adventurous young lady. I might even be coaxed into casting a sound-baffle spell to mask your snoring!"

"Do as you will, but leave my purse and King's oats alone. King must eat, and I don't want the lucre of filthy gold to tarnish your pure soul."

"Knock it off, you two," Molly said. "I'm going to get some sleep."

"He started it," Eric said helpfully.

"Good *night*, Eric! Or good whatever. I'm exhausted from riding. Oh, my aching — I'm sleeping on my stomach."

"Lucky for you we're only walking the ponies," Toby yawned, rolling out his sleeping mat. "It gets much more painful when you trot or gallop."

"I *have* been riding for a few months now," Molly groaned. "I just haven't been in the saddle for that long all at once before. Go to sleep, *please.*"

Night fell again, painting the bright green landscape with blue and purple shadows as the little party made its way south once more. They left the shore of Lough Mask as it began to bend toward the west, and trekked through the open space under the stars. A few tell-tale fires marked where the village of Cong sprawled between the two lakes, and they moved past the twinkling lights to the edge of Lough Corrib beyond.

"We'll catch the road again," Toby whispered. "It's smoother there, less likely for the ponies to stumble. And we'll need to follow the road east to the castle."

Hours later they turned inland, trusting the ponies' footing in the dark and hoping to avoid others on the road. After several miles, the sky began to brighten and Molly picked out a sizable rise in front of them. "What is that?" she asked, pointing.

"Knockma Hill," Eric replied from his pouch.

"Is that where the castle is?" she asked.

"Castle Hackett lies at the base of the hill," Toby muttered. "Now comes the hard part."

"No, now comes the part where we hide again until nightfall. Remember the plan," Molly whispered. "Let's work our way around the bottom of the hill and look for a hideaway. And hurry, it looks like it's going to rain today."

As they made their way through the saplings and brush, Molly noticed a rock outcropping. She led the way to find if the rocks would provide a ledge or similar protection. The first few drops fell from the sky, cold and wet. Then Molly stopped short.

"I don't believe it. There's a cave here!"

"I had heard of caves around Knockma," Toby said. "I guess you found one. Lucky for us! Let's get inside; it looks large enough to shelter the ponies as well."

They led the ponies inside and stood, shivering, watching the rain fall lightly in the dawn light.

"I guess we need to sleep again," Molly finally said. "At least we'll be dry. We'll feed the horses, and bed down for the day." She took a deep breath. "We'll begin after sundown, as planned."

Molly and Toby slept soundly. When they awoke they found Eric in his leprechaun form standing in the cave entrance, watching the sunset splash colors across the sky. "Looking back to the east, we'd probably see a rainbow," he said brightly.

"Okay," Molly announced, "time to get this started. Does everyone know their part?"

"I know what I'm supposed to do, but — " Toby paused as Eric raised a finger to his lips.

The leprechaun pointed into the depths of the cave. As the sun dipped behind them, they saw a light glowing deep within their underground shelter.

"That's not sunlight," Toby whispered. "That looks like a lantern or a torch. Who could be in here with us?"

"Only one way to find out. Coming, boys?"

The trio moved slowly toward the light. Eric melted into his ferret form and scampered ahead into the shadows. Molly and Toby walked behind, trying not to stumble on the uneven rock floor. After a hundred yards, they came to a corner they could peek around.

Two men sat across from each other with a small table between them. Little carved pieces of ivory were arranged on a pattern of alternating light and dark squares painted on the table. The man facing away from them was a bit on the portly side, but was fairly well dressed. The other man was of average height and wore a traveling robe over his clothes, the hood pulled over his head. The cloth looked to be of good quality despite its worn look. A metal lantern perched on a ledge above them, lighting the little alcove well enough for their purpose.

"They're playing chess," Molly whispered.

The man in the traveling robe cocked his head, and then smiled. "Excuse me, Conor. We have guests." He pushed the hood back, revealing a head of glorious blond hair. His eyes flashed blue in the light before he turned to look at the children crouching in the shadows.

He smiled again. "Hello, Molly."

She froze, her heart in her throat. Then realization dawned on her, but it did not lessen her shock.

Molly stood up and took a step toward the players. "Fionn?" she said.

chapter seventeen

The King of Connaught

he smiled wider than before. "I'm flattered you remember. Ah, but for you it's only been — what, a few months?"

"Yeah, I guess. Fionn! I'm so glad to see you! Look at you, all grown up! Gosh, you were only thirteen the last time we were together! I tried to find the castle in Donegal, but no one knew where it was, and ..."

"Whoa! You were searching for Castle Tiarnach?"

"Well, of course, I was trying to get in touch with you because — "

"You thought I could help you get back home again." Fionn smiled and raised a finger to his lips when Molly tried to speak again. "It appears we have a bit to catch up on, you and I. Before we get to that, I think it would be good to have introductions all the way around."

Molly nodded, taking a deep breath. "Sure. This is Toby Bourke, and this is Eric," she said sweeping her arm toward her companions.

Fionn's eyes sparkled with delight. "Not *the* Tibbot-ne-Long, the only offspring of Richard-in-Iron Bourke and the redoubtable Grania O'Malley? The pleasure is mine, young man!" He bowed, grinning warmly at Toby who seemed a bit flustered by the sudden attention.

"And it's not every day that one introduces their pet ferret by name," Fionn continued in a whisper. Molly looked at Eric in alarm. "Keep your current form for a bit, my dear Eric, we will speak freely in a while. We have one more guest who may find leprechauns in his back yard a shock."

The rotund man at the chess table leaned forward, frowning as he tried to catch Fionn's whisper.

Fionn straightened and turned to him. "May I introduce Conor Kirwan, Lord of Castle Hackett."

Lord Kirwan brightened at the introduction and stood quickly to bow. "My pleasure. Any friend of Finvarra's is welcome here."

Molly paled. "Uh, Fionn, may I speak to you in private?"

As they stepped into the tunnel, Molly whispered urgently to him. "I have to trust you on this. We may have just blown our chance to rescue our friends. Your chess-playing buddy runs the castle where they are imprisoned!"

Fionn's smile grew wider. "Oh, you must mean the hostages they brought in a couple of days ago! An old man and a young boy? Don't shake your head like that, Molly, it's all right! Conor! I believe you may be of great service to my friends!"

"How so, Lord Finvarra?" Conor asked.

"I'm afraid my friends are unaware of recent events concerning who controls Castle Hackett. Would you be so kind as to explain the situation to them?" Fionn guided Molly by her elbow back into the light, despite her mimed protests.

Lord Kirwan glowered in disgust. "I'll explain, though it pains me. A month ago the English booted me and my family out of our own castle. It seems the almighty Royal-Pain-In-The ..."

"Just the facts, please, Conor."

"Very well. The Royal *Governor* and *President* o' Connaught had need o' my facilities. So he took them, at the point of a sword. Now I'm living in the countryside like a peasant."

Molly felt her heart lurch. "Then you're not working with the English?"

"Now why would I offer even a warm ale to those devils?" Lord Kirwan huffed. "They've brought in soldiers and fortified the place. It'll take a while to raise an army to drive them out."

Fionn caught Molly's eye and nodded. "Then you would have no objections to helping my friends retrieve a couple of recent prisoners from your previous estate's dungeon?"

Lord Kirwan looked from Molly to Toby in surprise, joy dawning on his face. "You've come to free those poor wretches? I'll give ye all the help I can, but that's a tall order. Two children against the English that 'ave been pouring in here ..."

"Information is all that they ask," Fionn said quietly. He walked to the chess board and moved a bishop across the squares. "Check, and checkmate in four. You see?"

Lord Kirwan studied the board as Fionn pointed out the inevitable. "I don't know why I bother, Finvarra, I never come close to beating you in this game. But I do enjoy your company, and my play improves against others!"

Fionn clapped him on the back. "Knowledge is king, my friend, and that is something you can share to our mutual advantage. *If* someone wanted to steal some prisoners out of Castle Hackett, it would be helpful to know the layout of the castle, the rooms, doors, staircases, windows, exits ..."

Kirwan looked up at him. "I know my castle like the back o' me hand! Where's some parchment? I'll draw it up for ye this instant!"

Several hours later, a cheerful Lord Kirwan left the cave for his peasant dwellings. Fionn gathered the chess pieces into a leather pouch, and Molly and Toby sat down close by.

"You're really the King o' the Fairies, as Molly said?" Toby asked in awe.

Fionn chuckled. "Tell me, Molly, have you told these two all of our secrets?" He pushed back his golden locks to reveal his pointed ears.

In an instant Eric transformed from ferret to leprechaun and knelt at Fionn's feet. "Your Majesty," he whispered.

Fionn laid his hand gently on the leprechaun's shoulder. "My, my, surely this is not the same Eric that you created at the Build-A-Leprechaun Store, Molly?"

"You never cease to amaze me," Molly said. "How did you guess that?"

"Recall that you poured that drop of whiskey to create Eric *before* I ate the Salmon of Knowledge. It was part of what I received."

Toby blinked. "You mean the Salmon o' Knowledge isn't just a children's fable?" He looked in turn at the King of the Connaught Fairies, Eric the leprechaun, and Molly O'Malley from four hundred years in his future. He sighed. "Never mind me. I'll get used to this eventually."

"One more thing, Molly, I believe there is something out of place," Fionn said. "You said you were searching for me at Castle Tiarnach — "

"Yes."

"— which means that you believe you are in Glimmer."

"Well, obviously ..." she stopped, her face suddenly distraught. "Oh, boy."

"Molly, I'm here because Knockma Hill is my seat in the *real* world. I come here to play chess with mortals, and generally keep in touch with goings-on outside Glimmer. Surely you must have had some inkling — ?"

The girl hung her head. "Eric did tell me this was the real world. I guess I didn't want to believe it, because I thought I could find you in Glimmer." She raised her chin and grinned. "But it doesn't matter now, because I've found you anyway! You can help me get back home to my own time, can't you?"

"I have no power to send you home." He raised his hand as Molly started to protest. "But I know someone who may be able to help. It might take a few days to find her."

Molly exhaled as her shoulders fell. "That's a start, anyway. Thank you! I'll just have to be patient. My parents must be going crazy since I disappeared."

"What about your plan, Molly?" Toby asked.

"Your plan?" Fionn perked up. "Tell me your plan."

Molly went over her plan in detail with everyone gathered around. Fionn stopped her only to ask questions now and then.

Twenty minutes later, Fionn stood and stretched. "Molly, you're amazing. It has risks, certainly, but I think it has a good chance to succeed, despite the odds." He took Molly's hand and helped her up. "You are without doubt the bravest human I have ever met. I have only one more piece of advice to share with you."

He raised her hand to his lips and kissed it gently, his blue eyes locked on her green. "Wait until tomorrow night to act. The night will be clear."

chapter eighteen

The Witch-Child

Sir Nicholas Malby poured himself a glass of red wine imported from Spain and propped his boots up on Conor Kirwan's best desk. Things were going exactly as planned.

He swirled his goblet, inhaling the sweet aroma before sipping. Setting his drink aside, he picked up a large hand-drawn map and looked it over once more. "So many islands, so many secret harbors. Secret no more, Grace O'Malley!" Laying the sheet of paper back on the table, he returned to his cup. "That O'Flaherty fool knows his coastline, but he's much too attached to that nit of a grandson. The old man broke before any of the lad's fingers. Shame. I was looking forward to that part." He swilled the remainder of the wine and sighed with satisfaction.

He frowned at a commotion from the floors below. Malby rose and walked to the staircase leading down from the study. "What's going on down there?" he bellowed.

"Sir, a girl has presented herself and demands to see your Lordship! She claims — perhaps you should see for yourself, sir!" a voice answered.

"Idiots," Malby mumbled. "Bring her up, then! If this isn't important, you'll be sharing a cell with our guests!" He stepped back into his office, muttering curses as he refreshed his wine glass.

Shuffling feet on the flagstones and a rap at the door announced the visitors. Malby breathed deep, ready to frighten this ignorant girl with a well-deserved curse for bothering the Governor — no, *President* — of this godforsaken land. Instead he froze, leaving his oath unspoken.

This was no peasant girl. She wore a flowing blue gown, exquisite ruffles lending it a rich fullness. A clasp pulled her red hair behind her head to flow down her back, while her green eyes flashed with impatience. Impatience, not fear. An Irish girl, no doubt of it, and of some status. But most startling, she appeared to be only about twelve years of age.

"Sir Nicholas Malby," she said forcefully, "thank you for granting me an audience. I am here on behalf of Grania O'Malley, Queen of Connaught, to offer myself as a hostage for Myles and Seamus O'Flaherty, whom you have taken prisoner. My mistress feels it unbecoming for you to hold an old man and a child, so she is offering me as a fair substitute."

Malby took a sip of courage and found his voice. "And why should I be interested in you? You're naught but a child yourself, and no one of note."

The girl tilted her head slightly, and when she raised it again her green eyes bore into Malby's. "I am Molly O'Malley, a cousin to Grania and much beloved. You wish to avoid trouble with my Queen; I humbly recommend that keeping *me* as your hostage will foster goodwill between our peoples and avoid unnecessary conflict."

"Search her," Malby barked.

Molly bristled as the soldiers patted down the fluffy folds of blue cloth but stood still until they were done. "Nothing on her, sir."

"Your *queen* is a pirate and a revolutionary, and cannot be trusted." Malby leered at Molly. "You are well-coached, but I know Grace O'Malley for what she is."

"I would not presume to threaten your Lordship, but it *would* be more advantageous to have Grania O'Malley as an ally rather than as an enemy." Molly's voice was almost sing-song.

"You would not threaten — guards! Don't you have posts to attend to? Leave us!" He slammed his drink down on the desk, splashing droplets of red liquid across the papers lying there. Swearing, he blotted the map carefully with a lace handkerchief while the guards backed from the room. When it was mostly dry, he looked up to find the girl standing next to him.

"What's this?" she asked.

He snorted. "This, my little urchin, is what will bury your precious queen. Too long has Grace O'Malley raided our shipping, and when pursued, melted into the dratted Irish coastline. After she was released from Dublin prison, a fleet was sent to deal with her. They failed in their mission, however."

"I know," Molly said softly. "I was there. I watched the English run back to their ships. You should start a track team."

Malby glared at her. "I was in England at the time. When I returned to Connaught, I set new plans in motion. Now you see the result!" He took his dagger, gleaming silver with a gilded hilt and slammed the point into the wooden desk top. "I can track your pirate and her vermin-infested crew wherever they flee! She *will* acknowledge England as the rightful ruler in Ireland and Elizabeth as her Queen!"

"Perhaps, some day," Molly murmured. "But not from any of your scheming. Queen Grania has more connections than you know of. You should be wary of crossing her. Sir Nicholas, I implore you to accept Grania's offer while you still can. Release your prisoners and accept me as your hostage!"

He stood, his beard quivering. "I *will* take you as a hostage, but I will not release the prisoners! You have no power here. All you have accomplished is to give me more bargaining power. You have failed as a negotiator just as your people will fail to keep their pitiful independence."

Another commotion from below intruded. This time an armored guard clanked up the stairs double-time and flung the door open. Malby turned on him, livid. "What?"

"Begging your pardon, sir, but there's been ... there's been ..."

"Out with it, you buffoon!"

The guard gulped. "One of the prisoners is missing, sir."

"Impossible. There's no way that — " he looked at Molly and found her smirking at him.

"Maybe you should go check that out," she grinned.

An uncontrolled gurgle came from Malby's throat. He tramped to the stairs and growled to the guard, "Stay here, and make sure she doesn't get through this door! There's no other exit down. I'll return shortly." He put his back to the troublesome girl and descended the steps to the arguing voices below.

The dungeon was small, built for the occasional rule-breaker rather than political enemies, but it seemed sufficient to hold an old man and a boy. Malby stormed into the cellar and peered through the bars.

"He's been like that, guvnor, ever since we got back from taking that girl to you! Just staring, not moving, like he's under a spell!" The guard's eyes darted around as if looking for demons.

Malby swore. "Where's the boy?"

"Vanished, sir. Like smoke up a chimney."

"Impossible! He must be hiding in here somewhere! Open these bars!"

Keys quickly opened the lock and the iron door creaked open. Malby strode over to where Myles sat motionless, his eyes glazed and fixed on a point across the room.

"All right, you worthless piece of sea-garbage! Where is he? Where's your grandson? Tell me or you'll meet the frayed end of a flogging whip!" Malby's spittle flecked the old man's face.

Myles didn't even flinch. Enraged, Malby slapped the grizzled cheek hard and immediately howled in pain. The old man disappeared at the contact, and an oak timber clattered to the floor in his place.

Malby hopped back as if burned, holding his stinging hand. "Sorcery," muttered a guard. "He's turned into a piece of enchanted wood, he has."

Malby's saliva now spattered his own beard as he stared in disbelief at the scene. His breathing came fast and shallow. Then he lifted his eyes toward the ceiling. "That girl. That cursed Irish girl!" He raced from the dungeon and up the stairs.

When he reached the top, the guard was at his post outside the door. "Sir, she didn't come through here, as ordered," he offered.

"Open that door, you idiot!" Malby screamed.

The guard leaned on the door, but it didn't budge. He battered it with his shoulder, receiving only bruises for his efforts. "She's braced it from the inside, sir!"

"Get an axe, get something!" Malby cried, hysterical. "I want that door open!"

It felt like an eternity before more soldiers arrived with an axe and began chopping at the dark wood. Splinters flew. The door flexed with the impact. Finally the door gave way and they pushed past the chairs wedged against the entry.

The room was empty. Malby found his dagger still embedded in the desk top. He reached for the hilt to yank it from the wood, but he paused, shaking. He gasped.

The map was gone.

A small door stood slightly ajar across the room, inviting him. It led to the roof, and he knew there was no way off. Malby chuckled softly. He had her. He smiled at the thought of her panic, helpless to escape his grasp. *Was there ever any doubt that it would end differently?* Malby stepped up to view the parapet, open to the night sky.

Molly O'Malley stood on the castle wall, barefoot. Her fine blue dress was gone, and she wore a loose black cloak, all in tatters, that fluttered in the night breeze. She glanced down at Malby, a smug, confident look that made his blood boil. Then she lifted her face to the wind and closed her eyes, her unfettered red hair blowing behind her. A shadow covered her briefly, like a passing falcon, and she was gone.

Nicholas Malby stood on the stairway in silence for perhaps twenty seconds. Then he slowly walked back down to the study.

"Sir! Is she up there, sir?"

"Leave me," he croaked hoarsely.

The soldiers clanged out of sight as Malby poured himself another glass of wine. This glass he downed all at once, then hurled the goblet to shatter in the fireplace. The flames flared hungrily as they devoured the alcohol, and Malby collapsed into his chair as the fire returned to normal, sending shadows dancing across his face.

He covered his eyes and muttered wearily to himself: "How am I going to explain to the Queen that the witch-child, Molly O'Malley, willingly allowed herself to be carried off by a winged demon into the night?"

chapter nineteen

Doon Hill

Molly opened her eyes and blinked as the wind pounded her face. She squinted to keep from tearing and found herself looking down at Knockma Hill shrinking below. Her arms were pinned closely, but not uncomfortably to her sides. Still, she couldn't roll over. She craned her neck as far as she could to look up.

The great black dragon's wings beat a steady *one-and-a-two* as they climbed. The beast looked down at the frail parcel cradled in her razor-sharp talons. She carefully rolled Molly to her back so the girl could see the dragon more easily.

"Nefra," Molly breathed, "I knew you would come for me. The summoning spell that Eric cast worked perfectly. For that matter, so did the plan — at least, so far."

Nefra tilted her head to the side, puzzled. She trilled softly, a sound that rippled up from deep within her scaled chest.

"Oh, that's right. Sorry, Nefra. I hope this part works." Molly frowned for a moment, concentrating. *"TOO-war may gah jih BUN-ah-wen.* Did I say that right, Nefra? Did you understand? Take me to Bunowen!"

"Bunowen," the dragon repeated, and pivoted in the sky to chart a new course.

Though it was a moonless night, Molly's eyes had adjusted to the velvet darkness on the parapet of Castle Hackett, and she was able to pick out some features below them as they flew. "That looks really flat down there. Oh, I see, it's a lake! And an island! That must be Lough Corrib that Toby told me about, the one we traveled alongside for most of the night."

"Lough Corrib," Nefra agreed.

Molly looked up at the dragon again. "You can understand some of what I say. Let's try this." She freed one arm and pointed down, thrusting her finger again and again at the rocky island floating in the lake below them. "Change of plans, Nefra. Take me to the island. *TOO-war may gah jih* **island**. Please, Nefra, look where I'm pointing! The island!"

Nefra looked away into the distance, then down at the dark island surrounded by darker water. She hovered for a moment, and then dived in a shallow spiral toward the island. The landing was smooth and controlled, with only a slight scattering of pebbles as the dragon gripped the limestone.

"Great! Now let me down, dear — Nefra, you can let me go now — that's a good girl, thank you!" Molly carefully slipped to the ground avoiding the talons. "Oh, I wish I could tell you everything, but I can't! You see, I don't have the medallion right now."

She looked up wistfully into the dragon's eyes. Nefra scratched at her own scaly neck. "That's right, Nefra, I'm not wearing the medallion!" Molly smiled, patting her own neck, and then she threw her arms open. "I couldn't risk losing it, and I knew that the English would probably search me when I went to the castle, so I left it with Toby."

Molly slid the tattered black cloak over her head and spread it out on the ground. "Boy, has *this* ever come in handy. *Water."* The cloak shimmered in the starlight, and Molly patted the fabric softly. "Here it is," she murmured, and ran her fingernail along the cloak. The cloth parted easily as though cut, and the girl pulled out a folded paper from the interior pocket.

"Okay, this is important." Molly walked several feet away and laid the paper on the ground. "Nefra, this is a map that *must* be destroyed. Can you burn it, Nefra? You know, breathe fire?" The girl puffed out her cheeks and blew air on the paper, her arms stretched wide.

Nefra looked at the girl curiously. Molly was now dancing up and down, bobbing her head as she blew on the offending item. At last the dragon nodded and chuckled. Molly looked up at her, gasping for breath.

The black dragon stepped over to the map and stretched her wings in a wide arc to surround the area. Molly tried to poke her head around to watch, but Nefra gently pushed her back with her wing, while shaking her frilled head. Nefra bent her head close to the map and blew gently. The reek of sulfur filled the air, then with a flash the dragon's breath erupted into a torrent of devouring flame, charring the paper to ash in a second.

Nefra withdrew her protective circle and allowed Molly to examine the remains. "Awesome," Molly nodded. "That's taken care of. Now we need to get back to Bunowen."

"Bunowen?" Nefra asked, her eyes twinkling.

"Yes, Bunowen, and I mean it this time. Sheesh, you can certainly say a lot without talking." Molly grinned. She pointed to the spot behind Nefra's head. "Can I ride on your back the rest of the way instead of being carried?"

Nefra extended a powerful leg, and Molly scrambled to gather her cloak. She pressed the gash closed with a gentle pinch and whispered *"Ice."* The cloak returned to its former appearance, with no sign of the opening Molly had made.

Molly pulled the cloak over her head and scaled Nefra's leg to her back. She seated herself just behind a large ridge spike forward of the wings. "Okay, Nefra," Molly breathed. "Ready when you are."

The dragon crouched for a moment, and then sprang into the air with a massive downbeat of her wings. Molly held tight to the spike, but Nefra's momentum kept her firmly in position. The little island shrank behind them as they swept toward the stars.

Nefra flew across the lake, returning to her previous flight path. Ahead Molly could see mountains rising up, and less hilly ground to the left that met the sea. "Nefra, is that water over there Galway Bay?"

Nefra turned her head to the side for a moment. *"Galway ba,"* she said.

"Then that must be Connemara ahead of us?"

"Is ea, Connemara."

They traveled along the edge of the mountains, using them as a guide. Molly tugged her cloak closer as the wind chilled her. She fought to stay awake as an hour and more slipped by.

Then Nefra wheeled toward the bay.

Molly jarred herself awake. The shore seemed to be one huge cliff-line, white foam pounding the land in an unending crescent. Before them the land ended, and a vast ocean stretched out into the darkness. To their right rugged mountains marked the highlands. Then she saw the beach.

The secluded inlet looked as if it had been scooped out of the surrounding cliffs by a titanic server from a giant ice cream parlor. At the furthest point inland the sand lay flat and smooth, suitable for galleys to land. A castle emerged from the darkness, its towers and walls commanding the area close to the harbor. But Molly was looking for something else, and at last she spied it, rising like a great loaf of bread across the bay.

"Put us down there, Nefra! On top of the hill! It's Doon Hill, just as Toby said!"

Nefra followed Molly's hand signals and landed easily on the crest of the hill which dominated the area. Even the castle seemed insignificant by comparison. Molly climbed down the dragon's arm and hugged the great black neck.

"Oh, you did it, you beautiful thing! You brought me to Bunowen!"

"Bunowen," Nefra agreed with a pleased growl.

"I wish we had had the time to talk beforehand, when I still had the medallion! But it's all right, you understood enough to bring me here. I know you still can't understand me, but I need to talk to someone! Can I tell you, Nefra?" Molly patted the blue stripe that ran the length of Nefra's otherwise black body. The dragon sighed and lay down on the hilltop, folding her wings close.

"After Richard Joyce tried to kill me, I knew I had to do something," Molly said. "I couldn't let Grania walk into a trap. So I worked out a plan with Toby to rescue Myles and Seamus from the English. Richard had let it slip that they were at Castle Hackett.

"My idea was to offer myself as a hostage to Governor Malby. That would create a diversion so that Toby and Eric could sneak in and get Myles and Seamus out. Then when they discovered that Myles and Seamus had escaped, that would be the diversion to get *me* out. That's where you came in. I summoned you from the roof of the castle, and you swooped down and carried me away. Sir Nicholas Malby will have nightmares for weeks, I hope." She fingered the silver heart-shaped locket around her neck. "I hid this in my shoe, because I needed the shamrock inside to summon you. But the medallion is too big and heavy to escape a search, which I figured they would do. So I had to leave it with Toby."

Molly smiled. "You're smart. Even though I had Toby teach me a little Irish to tell you to take me to Bunowen, you understood other things, like landing on that island. If we tried to burn the map on top of this hill, everyone would know we're here. You still need to stay hidden. And I can't be discovered yet. Not just yet."

She drew a shaky breath and continued. "That's where the plan gets a bit more complicated. We knew that a couple of horses could probably sneak past the extra English forces, since they were looking for Grania and a whole army. So Toby was going to put Myles and Seamus on Duchess and send them straight back north to Rockfleet."

Nefra looked confused. "I know, dear, you don't understand a word of this, maybe a few place names that sound the same. Anyway, the English wouldn't be chasing Myles and Seamus because Toby was going to lead the English the other direction, riding King. Toby is supposed to ride south, cross the inlet north of Galway City into Connemara, and ride here to Bunowen, to meet us and give me back the medallion. Only ..." she glanced back the way they had come ... "it's a terribly long way."

She looked up at Nefra as if pleading. "We only walked the horses coming down, because they had to be rested for their rides tonight. Both of them will be pushed to their limits. And we needed to take a couple of days to reach Castle Hackett, because you needed those days for your wing to heal. I guess it did. Lucky for me!"

Nefra seemed to nod. *Or was she falling asleep?* Molly thought. "It was a good piece of luck finding Fionn as we did. Who knew that his otherworld seat in the real world was right there under Knockma Hill? He was a big help, getting Conor Kirwan to give us the complete plans to the castle so we could plan our moves. And Fionn helped me make the dress, too. I had a swatch of the beautiful dress that the O'Donnell gave me in Donegal, and we used it to train the magic cloth to match the color and texture. He's actually pretty good with fixing hair, too, but that's to be expected after eating the Salmon of Knowledge, I guess."

Molly pulled the edge of her cloak to her cheek. "After that Malby guy ran downstairs to check on the prisoners, I wedged chairs against the door. Then I changed the dress into this cloak. I made a pocket in it and put my shoes and the map inside, then sealed it completely so nothing could fall out when you grabbed me. Man, that was lucky that he had the map right in the room! There were so many things that *could* have gone wrong. And maybe there are still some things that did go wrong that I don't know about yet." The girl whispered *"Water"* and unzipped the secret pocket again to retrieve her shoes, closing it afterward. She slipped her flats onto her feet and stood up.

"Nefra, you need to go. Toby has Eric with him to create diversions and all kinds of mischief so they can escape the English and get here safely. I *hope* they'll be all right. But it will be morning soon, and *you* need to find a big, dark hiding place." She rubbed the black muzzle fondly. "Go on, now, I'll be fine."

Nefra nuzzled her softly, her yellow eyes sad. "Go!" Molly whispered, blinking back tears as she pointed to the mountains. The dragon released a puff of steam from her nostrils in resignation, and then turned and vaulted into the night sky. She vanished almost immediately, her passage marked only by groups of stars that disappeared and then twinkled back into existence.

Molly sat down on Doon Hill and drew her cloak around her. She played with the fringe, closing the strips back together for warmth and a more conventional look. Fionn had suggested the tatters — apparently they worked from the brief expression she glimpsed on Governor Malby's face.

She jumped as she felt her head bob. The sky was lighter, and the sun was peeking over the horizon from the direction of Lough Corrib. How long had she slept? She yawned and stretched her aching muscles.

Something moved on the road, far away. The road ran along the foot of the mountains, and would branch to bring travelers to Bunowen Castle along the left fork.

Molly stood to get a better look. It was a rider, on a black horse. Still moving fast at a steady gallop. Who would gallop a horse at this time of the morning? She bit her lip in excitement. Could it be — ? The rider took the left fork, bypassed the castle and cantered across the fields to the foot of Doon Hill. A young form dropped limply from the saddle to the ground.

But Molly was already racing down Doon Hill, running and sliding as rapidly as she dared. Toby had come at last.

chapter twenty

Owen of Bunowen

ric was already his leprechaun self, checking Toby carefully as Molly rushed up. "Is — is he all right?" she gasped.

"The lad's exhausted, and the pony as well," Eric said with some concern. "They both need immediate attention."

Molly cradled Toby's head, and his eyes opened a crack. "Is that you, Molly? You're safe, then! Your plan ... worked ..." His eyes fluttered and closed.

"Toby! You stay with me! You're going to be all right!" she whispered, fresh tears sliding down her cheeks.

His eyes opened again. "Oh, yes, I'll be all right. And I kept my end of the bargain. Take this ... this ..." He struggled with a gold chain around his neck.

"The medallion!" Molly said. "Let me help you with that!" She carefully lifted the chain over Toby's head. The stone disc looked the same as it did before, dark and cold in the starlight. She traced the combination of rough and polished patterns on the surface with her finger. "Thank you, Master Bourke; I'll be needing that now!" Molly dropped the necklace over her own head, carefully tucking the medallion inside her shirt.

"You're welcome," he mumbled, and fell asleep.

Molly gathered Eric up in a big hug. "Oh, I'm so glad you're both okay! Did you free Myles and Seamus?"

"Aye, it all went just as ye planned — oof! Enough hugging, girl, if ye want the story!"

She set him down gently. "Yes, but hurry. We have to take care of Toby and King."

"When ye made your grand entrance into the castle, the guards were distracted enough to let Toby slip in. I changed into a wee mouse so I could squeeze through the bars. I unlocked the cell door with a spell, and then Toby came up and pretended to open the door."

"So they didn't see you?"

"Not a crimson hair. Once Toby had them out, I set up a piece o' wood and enchanted it to take Myles' place. It was as lifelike as the real thing, I'd say — looked exactly like he does when he dozes off after one o' Dierdre's fine meals."

"And then you crawled out the window while Toby put Myles and Seamus on Duchess?"

"Exactly. Then Toby and I lit out south on King to draw the soldiers after us, so Myles could escape back north to Rockfleet."

"You must have had a terrible ride. King looks awful, and Toby — well, he's passed out already." She pulled a curry brush from the saddle bag and began working the dirt and sweat from King's ebony coat.

"I rode behind young Toby, casting spells back at our pursuers! I tell ye, Molly, lightning came from the pony's ar — "

"Now, Eric, are you sure that's really what happened?" She carefully lifted King's tail to check.

"Well, some sparks, anyway. Didja know that when summoned, a colony o' bats flying into the faces of pursuing riders can be highly effective in dampening their enthusiasm?"

"Eew. I'm glad you're on *our* side. I think. What should we do next?"

"For starters, I'll be needin' a hiding place," Eric grinned. "Look to the castle, we've got company!"

She turned to see four people walking from the castle toward them. "Ooh, you're right! Let's get you undercover!" She quickly transformed the cloak into her carrying pouch and a white ferret was soon curled up comfortably in the pocket.

Molly stood to greet their welcoming — she hoped — committee. The lead person in the group, wearing a rust-red doublet and white leggings, reached her first. "Good morning! We saw the horse ride past this morning without stopping and decided to see what brings visitors out so early. Is your — friend all right?"

"Thank you sir — he needs help! He's exhausted from a long ride, and his pony, too!" Molly said. "We're looking for Owen O'Flaherty — do you know where he is?"

The man stooped over Toby and gently turned his face toward him. "Toby!" he exclaimed. "Tomas, Brian, help me carry him to the castle! Peadar, grab the pony's bridle, will you? Quickly!"

"You know him?" Molly asked, wide-eyed.

"I should think I would know my own brother! I'm Owen O'Flaherty! Who are you, that's looking after him so poorly?" He winked at her to show he meant no harm by his remark, and then cast a worried look at Toby as they lifted him and started for the castle.

"I'm — Molly O'Malley," she managed. "You're Grania's oldest son?"

"Aye," he grunted as they walked toward the grey castle. "I imagine we're related in some way, then?"

"I would imagine," Molly agreed softly.

"This pony looks like he's been ridden hard," Peadar observed. "Ye didn't both come on him, did ye?"

"No, I had my own pony. But we got separated, and Duchess went off a different direction," Molly said. *And that's the truth,* she thought.

"Lucky she got you here before she ran off. Oof, this brother o' mine has been growing like a weed since I saw him last." Owen readjusted his grip on Toby's limp form.

As they approached the gate, several more people ran out to meet them, gently hoisting the boy from his bearers and carrying him the rest of the way. Owen walked beside them, motioning for Molly to keep up.

"Have you been riding all night?" he asked. "That's crazy! One misstep in the dark and your pony could break a leg, or throw you and break your neck!"

"It couldn't be helped," Molly replied earnestly. "We were pursued by the English."

"The English? What did you do?"

"What does anyone have to do except be Irish?"

He smiled grimly at her. "Aye, that's the truth. How did you lose them?"

"You'll have to ask Toby that when he wakes up. Maybe they weren't up for a chase in the middle of the night. I know I didn't get stopped when I went by."

Owen furrowed his brow. The party stepped inside the outer walls. They hurried Toby to the main quarters while Peadar led King to the stables for a rubdown, water and rest.

"That's one heck of a ride," Owen said when Toby was settled in Owen's own bed. "How far did you say you came?"

"I didn't say," Molly said carefully, putting on what she hoped was a relaxed smile. "Toby came from just east of Galway City. I had a little head start on him, so I'm not *quite* as tired as he is." She yawned and stretched for effect. "I'm still bushed; I'm not used to riding that far. Toby's a fine horseman, you know."

Owen scratched his short beard. "Yes, I know. Why don't we find a place for you to lie down, unless you're hungry or thirsty?"

Molly shook her head. "Just a bed sounds great. I'm bringing my pet ferret in with me. His name is Eric."

Owen laughed. "I had a pet mouse when I was little. Granuaile told me she didn't care what I did with it as long as I didn't bring it aboard ship. 'Enough rats on board already, and who will be able to tell the difference?' she said. I still don't know if she was talking about the real rats or the sailors."

"That sounds like Grania," Molly giggled.

She soon found herself sinking into a deep feather mattress down the hall from Toby. It felt heavenly compared to the cold night on Doon Hill, and she quickly fell fast asleep.

———

Molly woke to the smell of hot sausage and eggs. She rubbed her eyes and sat up.

A young woman with golden hair, dressed in a plush green gown, stood at her bedside. A small boy next to her held a tray of food. "Good morning, Molly," the woman said. "I am Brigid, wife to Owen O'Flaherty. Would you like some breakfast?"

"Yes, thank you, I'd love breakfast."

The boy set the tray on Molly's lap. "Would you like something to drink, Miss?" he asked.

"If it's not too much trouble, do you have any buttermilk?"

"I'll fetch a cup immediately, Miss." The boy nodded and hurried from the room.

"My son, Dónal. He's a good lad, like his father." Brigid smiled after him. "Would you like me to leave while you eat?"

"Oh, no, please stay if you would. I'd like someone to talk to, and Toby needs his rest." Molly picked up her knife and spoon. She had almost gotten used to not having a fork over the past several months.

"As you wish." Brigid seated herself on a nearby ottoman. "How long have you known Toby?"

"I met him last March," Molly said between bites. "It was great having someone my age to hang around with."

"It sounds like you two had quite an adventure."

"Yeah, but the most important part isn't over yet. Not until I know that Myles and little Seamus have made it safely back to Rockport."

"Myles O'Flaherty?" a voice boomed from the doorway. "Surely he's not still causing trouble?" Owen leaned against the door jamb, a smile creasing his face.

"You know Myles?" Molly asked.

"I was nearly twenty when Granuaile sailed back to Umhall with two hundred O'Flaherty sailors, including Myles," he said. "Yes, I remember him. Oh, and Toby might have mentioned something about him just a minute ago before he fell asleep again."

"Toby's awake?"

"Finish your breakfast, Molly; he came to for only a few minutes. You were saying that Myles was heading back to Rockfleet?" Owen put his arm gently around his wife's shoulders.

"Yes, the plan was for Myles and Seamus to ride back to Rockfleet while Toby and ... uh, King, led the English south. Toby's real goal was to come to Bunowen, to meet up with me. We figured we'd be safe here." She waved a piece of sausage around on the tip of her knife.

"I won't feel safe until you eat that bit o' meat and set the knife down!" Owen chuckled. "Ho, what have we here?"

Dónal stepped past his father, concentrating on the edge of a nearly-full glass. "Buttermilk," he said soberly.

"Thank, you — Dónal, is it?" Molly smiled and accepted the glass from him, taking a big slurp of the creamy liquid. "Mmm... that's so good."

"I don't think the English will be battering down our doors any time soon." Owen said. "They don't like the O'Flahertys."

"If they don't like you, wouldn't that make it more likely that they would attack you?"

"You don't know about the west gate?" Brigid laughed. Molly shook her head. "The brave citizens of Galway City have inscribed upon their western gate — the side facing Connemara — the words 'From the ferocious O'Flahertys, Good Lord deliver Us.' I don't think we need to worry just yet."

She reached out and grasped her husband's hand. "I must go tend to the affairs of the home now. I trust my husband will not tire you overmuch with idle chatter."

"I will be the perfect host, my love," Owen smiled. "Run along, Dónal my boy. I want to talk with our guest for a bit, and I don't think it can possibly qualify as idle chatter."

Mother and son moved off down the hallway. Owen's deep brown eyes twinkled. "So now that you've met up with Toby, what's the next part of your plan?"

"We wait — and rest. Toby especially had a hard ride to get here."

"Wait for what?"

Molly looked surprised. "You really don't know?"

Owen shook his head, obviously puzzled.

"When Myles shows up back at Rockfleet and tells Grania where Toby is, do you think she's going to just sit there?"

"Ah! Of course! Granuaile will set sail with all possible haste to come here." Owen nodded. "You seem to have this thought out in some detail. Is this all *your* plan, Molly?"

"Mostly." She took another bite of sausage. "But we all had to work together to pull it off." She scratched Eric's furry white head as he snuggled beside her. The ferret yawned and went back to sleep.

"Well, I'm impressed. You kids have done some amazing things. Get your rest. Toby seems to be doing fine. He should be up and around in a day or so. I think I'll go check on King."

Three days later, Molly and Toby sat on the rock wall overlooking Bunowen harbor. Eric climbed onto Molly's shoulder to view the azure waves that lapped the beach.

"Do you think he made it?" Molly whispered.

"I don't know. I sure hope so. We couldn't have done any more," Toby sighed. "It seemed like there were sixty riders chasing after me. Myles only needed to wait in the cave for an hour before setting out. Surely drawing the watch after me would help him get away."

"If he didn't make it, if he was recaptured, then everything we did was for nothing! We'd be right back where we started, with Sir Malby forcing Myles to draw him another map." Molly sighed and brushed a tear away. "We won't know until we see Grania sail into this harbor."

Eric stiffened on her shoulder and hissed. Molly started, and then followed the ferret's gaze out to sea.

A fleet of ships rounded Doon Hill's bulk, their billowing sails taut with the favorable westerly wind. The red boar of the O'Malleys flew boldly from the mast of the lead galley, and the caravel *Banshee* sliced through the *Margaret's* wake. The *Black Oak* and the *Sea Witch* guarded the rear, their oars churning the blue surface white as the convoy swept toward the little bay.

"I hope Mam won't be too mad at us," Toby gulped.

chapter twenty-one

Overboard

*g*ranuaile leaped into the surf before the *Margaret's* prow slid all the way onto the golden sand. She strode up to the children, her blue eyes darkening to indigo as a cloud covered the sun. "I want some answers, and I want them now!" she hissed, her bosom heaving.

Molly stepped in front of Toby. "I owe you that much," she said, feeling her stomach knot up. "But first, did Myles get back okay?"

Granuaile glared at the red-haired girl for a moment. "He's on the deck o' the *Banshee* right now. Came out o' nowhere with a story about children stealing him right out from under the noses of the English army. And something about a map."

Molly took a deep breath. "You don't have to worry about the map. I burned it. It's gone."

"You?" The dark-haired queen's eyes widened. "Molly O'Malley, the lost girl without parents, pulling my son into dangerous adventures across two counties? This was your idea, then?"

"Yes. And you want to know why." Molly sighed. "Remember the man who attacked me at Elva's place?"

"Yes, Richard O'Kelly."

"His real name was Richard Joyce. He went there to kill me because I recognized him from the night of the kidnapping."

"Why didn't ye tell me, child, we could have ..."

"I couldn't tell you! He was talking, bragging about what he and the English planned to do to you! He *wanted* you to come after Myles at Castle Hackett. It was a trap! You would have been killed!"

"Well, nothing's a certainty now, is it?" Granuaile pursed her lips. "So you thought that two children could succeed where an army o' trained soldiers could not?"

Molly grinned. "They were prepared for an army. They weren't prepared for us."

"Apparently not. Toby," she said, turning her attention to the trembling boy, "are you also going to tell me that this plan was hatched by this girl? That you had no part in it?"

"Well, I knew the way to the castle." He managed a faint smile.

"And he rode all the way across Connemara in one night," Molly added proudly.

"I need a flagon of ale," the queen said, touching her temple. "All this talking is making my head buzz."

"I'm sure Owen has plenty in his cellar. Why don't we head to the castle and sit down?" Toby suggested.

More men were arriving from the galleys, which had all beached themselves now. A longboat from the *Banshee* rowed steadily toward the shore. Molly recognized a familiar balding head on one of the occupants. "Myles," she whispered.

"By all means, let's wait until Myles joins us," Granuaile muttered. "He doesn't drink that much, or I wouldn't have believed his wild tale."

Oh, Grania, we've not told you half of this wild tale, Molly thought. *You wouldn't believe us if we did.*

"More ale, Mother?" Owen smiled.

"No, dear boy, I need my head clear to sail back tonight," Granuaile growled.

"Wait — we're going back tonight?" Toby gasped. "But you just got here!"

"If this is a trap, as Molly says, those English might just march across Connemara and attack Bunowen. We should get back to Rockfleet where I have three hundred gallowglass to discourage them. Staying here only endangers Owen." Granuaile set her cup down on the smooth wooden table.

"Mother, I hardly think — "

"Yes, Owen, I know, and that's the problem. Not everyone in Connemara is a 'ferocious O'Flaherty' who will step in front of an English force. Certainly not Murrough of the Battle Axes, who sold his sacred Gaelic birthright for an English pedigree of nobility! He would join them if he thought it would benefit him!"

Owen threw up his hands. "Go, then. Do you have a moment to kiss your grandson?"

Granuaile's smile stretched easily across her weather-beaten face. "Always. Where is Dónal?"

They tacked toward the west and the setting sun as they cleared Bunowen Bay. "We'll be home by late tomorrow, if the wind doesn't shift on us," Granuaile said, shading her eyes.

"King is in his stall below decks," Toby announced as he climbed to the forecastle. "I'm glad you brought the *Banshee*, it's hard getting a pony onto a galley."

"It's harder getting children to obey instructions," Granuaile grinned, her eyes twinkling. "Tell me again how you distracted the guards, Molly?"

"I demanded an audience with Sir Nicholas Malby and offered myself as a hostage in exchange for Myles and Seamus."

"You talked with Malby?"

"Yes, and he's a despicable man." Molly sniffed.

"Ahoy!" came a voice from the stern. "Ships behind us!"

The commander raced to the other end of the caravel and peered over the poop deck. Molly and Toby arrived behind her, breathless.

"English galleons, with their cursed scarlet crosses on the sails. Must have come out o' Galway. They're no threat; the wind is against them here. The galleys can outrow them and the caravel is more efficient at tacking." The pirate queen smiled and returned to the conversation. "It looks like your 'despicable man' is still chasing you, Molly."

The sunset dimmed behind thick, dark clouds that hovered just above the black sea. "Looks like it will be a compass night, Myles," Granuaile said to the navigator.

"Aye," Myles replied. "No stars to guide us, no sun to show the shore. I'll take us out to sea a bit further, in case the storm tries to drive us toward the coast."

"Ahoy! Ships to starboard!"

Granuaile whirled to see. Darkness was settling like a cloak, but the newcomers could be clearly seen against the rocky coastline.

"What is it, Grania?" Molly whispered, coming up beside her.

"Another trap, dear," the queen replied. "Barbary pirates, ten ships at least. They must have been hiding along the coast."

"We can outrun them, too, can't we?"

Granuaile shook her head. "They have galleys like we do. The wind will have little effect on them. We can't turn back; the English are driving us to the pirates."

She turned to her crew. "All hands, battle stations! Pirates to the starboard! Load the cannon!" Granuaile hurried toward the forecastle, pierced with gunports and bristling with artillery.

Toby started after his mother, and then stopped. "Molly, come on! We have to get you someplace safe!"

Molly stood on the high poop deck, staring into the darkening mist that was beginning to fall. "There is no place safe, Toby."

"Molly, get into the cabin! You've got to get off the deck!"

She padded slowly to the back of the ship and looked over the railing. The wake churned the water white as the *Banshee* leaned against the wind. "There are too many of them, even for Grania. Ten pirate ships, twenty English, to her four? It's impossible. They'll be here before the light fades completely." She lifted Eric from her pouch and set him gently on the deck. He cocked his head and blinked. "Stay with Toby, Eric."

"Molly, what are you doing?" Toby shouted.

She carefully opened her silver heart-shaped locket, making sure she grasped the green shamrock carefully in her hand. "The only thing I can do. Something unexpected."

Molly whispered into her fist.

"Out of time, out of myth,
I summon you now here forthwith.
Nefra, heir of the dragon race,
come now to this time and place."

She clicked the locket closed around the shamrock again and stepped up onto the railing, balancing herself by grasping a rope.

"Molly!"

She turned to view Toby's horrified face. "Goodbye, Toby." Then she shut her eyes and allowed herself to fall backward.

The water struck her like a cannonball, then the numbing cold hit. The surface closed over her head and she felt herself being sucked down, down into the murky waters below. *I wonder if Nefra will be able to find me in time,* she mused. Tiny bubbles floated up as she descended into the depths.

chapter twenty-two

Storms and Secrets

molly fought the urge to let her air go. Her chest hurt; it hurt worse than anything she'd ever felt before. The water was so dark, and getting darker …

Something even darker flashed by her.

I'm dreaming, Molly thought, *I'm going to drown any minute. I miss my family …*

A bump, a gentle but firm squeeze. Then the water rushing by her at incredible speed, a steady *push, push* propelling her through the brine.

Her lungs screamed in pain.

A change in direction. Molly felt herself being pulled deeper under the water. *No!* She silently screamed. *Nefra?*

Then the direction was sharply up, up, gaining speed …

Nefra broke the surface and rose with a massive downbeat of her wings into the air. In her talons Molly gasped and coughed as they flew toward the rocky shore.

They landed at the edge of the cliffs. Nefra set Molly gently on the ground, where the girl took shaky breaths, spitting out sea-water. After a minute Molly looked up at the dragon, who was waiting patiently for her.

"Could you have cut it any closer?" she wheezed.

"I'm sorry, Molly," the dragon said quietly. "You were harder to find in the water. I assumed that you wished me to find you there instead of on the deck of the ship."

Molly coughed again. "Did you see the other pirates? The ones coming out from the coast?"

Nefra pivoted her head out to sea. "I see them now. We swam under them before coming up for air. They are almost to Granuaile's fleet."

"We've got to help Grania. That's why I summoned you. We have to save her!" Molly began shivering.

"We've got to warm you up first. Stand right there." Nefra took a deep breath and blew over Molly. A sound like a furnace rumbled from deep within her, and Molly felt a blast of hot air slam into her. Quickly she pulled off her outer shirt and the magic cloth, holding them in the path of Nefra's giant blow dryer. They dried quickly and she rubbed her arms and legs, feeling the warmth return in seconds.

"Okay, that's good enough! We've got to go now!" Molly donned her clothing again. "Will you fly me out to the ships?"

"What will we do there?"

"You're going to use your fire-breath to set their sails on fire."

"Won't they see us?" Nefra extended a great foreleg to Molly.

"They'll see the fire, but we'll come out of the clouds at them. Sudden bright light will blind their night vision; they won't see anything but the flames. Maybe they'll think it's lightning." The girl scampered up the leg and took her seat on Nefra's neck. "Can you tell the difference between the Barbary pirate galleys and Grania's ships?"

"Flags are hard to see from above."

Molly furrowed her brow. "Grania said she couldn't outrun them because the African pirates had galleys, too. The wind wouldn't be enough of a factor. Oh — that's it! The pirates are coming out from the coast! They're going straight into the west wind! They won't want to mess with having their sails up when they can row straight out to the fleet, while Grania's ships are using their sails to catch the crosswind! Nefra, you just have to look for ships that have their sails furled, all tied up. They will be the bad guys. We'll set their masts on fire!"

"Whatever you say." Nefra launched herself off the cliff, stretched her wings to catch a thermal, and rose rapidly into the clouds.

"One more thing," Molly shouted. "Attack the ships at the rear first. Everyone is looking to the front at Grania. That way the ones at the front won't know they are being attacked until it's too late. I think Sergeant York did something like that in World War One when he attacked the Germans."

"I don't think I was supposed to know that," Nefra said cheerily.

"Oops! Sorry! Just attack them from the back! Just the sails! And leave a few of the ships at the front alone!"

"Why?"

"Most sailors can't swim. We need to leave a few ships able to rescue the survivors from the burned ships."

"Hmmm … I didn't think you liked these pirates?"

"I don't — but I don't want to kill people if there is any other way!"

"If that's what you want." The clouds thinned below them, revealing a cluster of galleys rowing with furled sales. "Hang on!"

Nefra dropped from the inky clouds like a bullet, silent as a hawk. Molly clung to the spike, trying to keep her eyes open in the stinging wind. Then the sky turned white in front of the dragon and Molly felt the heat trailing back to her. Nefra pulled up and disappeared into the clouds again. Molly risked a look over her shoulder and saw the galley still in the water, her mast and sails roaring like a giant torch. Bits of cloud rushed together and they flew in the darkness once more.

They wheeled together, dragon and rider as one, plummeting to leave behind something that resembled a giant candle on a floating birthday cake. Molly heard the cries of men, strange accents filled with terror that faded as they ascended into the thick clouds once more. Again they dove, billowing smoke from the burning ships now helping to hide their attack.

Molly fought the tears that sprang into her eyes, hoping fervently that the sailors jumping from their ruined ships would be rescued. She had tasted the teeth of the ocean once tonight, and she could not wish that on anyone.

"Enough!" Molly cried. "That's enough, Nefra! We've gotten seven of them, and the lead ships have turned back! They won't attack now."

The dragon lifted and banked away from the battle. She rose steadily until they tore through the ragged tops of the clouds. Nefra's great wings beat a rhythmic pace as they flew under the stars.

"Where are we going, Nefra?"

"Where do you want to go?"

Molly sighed. "This all happened so fast, I didn't have time to plan ahead. I can't go back to the ship, that's for sure. I guess — just take me back to Rockfleet."

The clouds scattered before they reached Clare Island. They soared along the north edge of Clew Bay and landed quietly a half-mile from Rockfleet. Molly climbed down and hugged Nefra's great head. "What will you say?" the dragon rumbled. "How can you explain what happened to you?"

"Beats me," Molly admitted. "Toby will know, but Grania ..." she shook her head.

"I'll leave you now. You have one summons left." Nefra winked one giant yellow eye. "Hopefully it won't be as exciting as the first two."

"I may need to use it to have you carry me away when Grania gets here," Molly sighed. "I don't know if she'll be angry, or frantic — no, Grania wouldn't be frantic. She's going to be mad. I don't know how much longer I can keep all of these secrets."

Nefra raised her head and sniffed the air. "I must leave. Be careful, Molly." The dragon sprang into the air and disappeared over the treetops.

"What if I decided to leave right now? Thanks a lot, Nefra!" she moaned. The girl turned and began trudging toward the castle.

She found the path and walked along in the starlight. Her clothes were still a little damp, and she shivered again as she headed toward Elva's and some dry clothes.

The night was quiet, with only the singing of the crickets competing with the sound of the waves lapping the shore of Clew Bay. Molly glimpsed Rockfleet towering above the last trees ahead and quickened her step.

As she neared the end of the woods, she stopped and held her breath. A figure stood in the shadow of the last tree. A dark cloak hid the stranger's features.

They stared at each other for a minute, neither moving. Then the figure stepped out into the path. A female voice spoke clearly: "Molly O'Malley? Don't be afraid, dear."

"Do — do I know you?" Molly asked.

"I believe you know a great deal, dear child. It's a burden for you to carry so many secrets."

"Who are you?" Molly demanded, taking a step backward.

"Come closer and see. Finvarra said you would be expecting me."

"Finvarra? Fionn sent you? Then you must be the one he mentioned, who could help me ..." She ran to the hooded figure, stopping ten feet away. "Who are you?"

The figure pushed her hood back. Her auburn hair framed her beautiful face, which Molly knew in an instant.

"Lioc! You sent Paddy and me back through time from Glimmer! Oh, can you send me back to my time now?"

The woman smiled. "Things are not that simple, Molly. You are here in the real world, changing — or preserving — your own history, as well as that of Grania O'Malley. There are a few things we need to take care of first. Beginning with the Queen of Connaught. We will wait for her to arrive, together."

"Are you sure that's a good idea?" Molly asked uncertainly. "Do you know Grania?"

"Better than you know. Your actions have saved Grania from an early demise, from Sir Nicholas Malby's traps on land and sea. In fact, I think you may have created a little superstition in his mind concerning her. Tell me, Molly, why did you do it?"

"They are all fighting, fighting to survive, holding on against incredible odds. It's so unfair. And Grania and Toby and Elva, they've all been so good to me ... they've shown me what courage is." She looked up, blinking back tears. "How could I not be as brave as they are?"

"Come here, Molly." The woman opened her arms and Molly rushed into her embrace, sobbing. They hugged each other tightly.

"Molly," the woman whispered. "I use the name Lioc at times when I walk the world. But my true name is Clio."

"C-Clio? Is — is that an anagram?"

Clio smiled. "Lioc is the anagram, with the letters rearranged from Clio. Now, one more thing. The medallion you wear?"

Molly nodded.

"It's *my* medallion, child. It's the key to getting you back home."

chapter twenty-three

Granuaile

Sir Nicholas Malby tugged nervously at his beard as he surveyed the carnage ahead.

The captain stepped up beside him and offered a burnished spyglass. "Care for a closer look, sir?"

"Hang it, Martin, it's obvious what's going on! Our pirate partners from the Barbary Coast are in flames, and the devil Grace O'Malley is going to run right by them while they're saving their own skins! How in blazes did this happen?"

Martin shrugged. "There is a storm approaching. I've never seen lightning like that before, though. And all in one place?"

"And only striking Grace O'Malley's enemies," Malby growled. "I've never believed in black magic before, but these past few days ..."

"Sir, the wind favors the Irish pirates. We'll not catch them before the storm hits. I recommend that we return to Galway." The captain looked out to sea, where the sky was clearly worsening.

Malby's knuckles whitened as he gripped the ship's rail. "Give the order, then. Return to Galway."

The captain barked an order, and then turned back to his master. "What will you do next, sir?"

Malby laughed hoarsely. "Next? Next? I suppose, my dear Captain Martin, that I will return to Roscommon." His eyes softened as he stared at the fires from the dying ships on the horizon. "I've been thinking about building an addition to the castle there."

"Sir, she is only a woman."

The President of Connaught looked at Martin through bleary eyes and nodded. "Yes, that's what some say." He left the quarterdeck with measured steps, heading for his quarters below.

Sparks filled the air, but the wind blew them back on the Barbary pirates. "Give us a bit more room, Myles," Granuaile breathed softly as she eyed the sky. The *Banshee* promptly turned slightly to port to put more water between the pirate fleets.

She looked at Toby, who trembled while he stroked the white ferret's head. "The fight's over, boy, the pirates are saving what's left o' their ships. We'll sail right past them. Are ya still afraid?"

He nodded. "Mam, it's Molly ..."

"Molly? Did ya get her below decks? Where is she, anyway?"

His voice choked. "She wouldn't listen to me, I told her to come down ..."

"Toby! Where is she?"

"She — she went overboard. She climbed up on the rail and just fell off."

"She slipped?"

"No, it wasn't like that. She just let herself fall backwards."

Granuaile's eyes were as dark as the midnight sea. "She wouldn't do that. Molly wouldn't give up! Not after everything she's done — "

Toby wiped his face with his sleeve. "It didn't look like she was giving up, Mam. I think she had another plan. She sent Eric to me." He rubbed his cheek on the ferret's head.

"A plan? Throwing yourself into the sea is not a plan, Toby! If those pirates hadn't ..." she stopped, gazing at the floating bonfires receding behind them.

"Toby!" she whispered fiercely, grabbing the boy by his shoulders. "Do ya mean to tell me you think Molly had something to do with those ships catching fire?"

"I don't know! I don't know for sure! But I wouldn't put it past her. Molly is — amazingly resourceful."

Granuaile looked behind the fleet. "It's getting too dark to see where the English are. We're past the pirates. I can only assume that if Molly planned anything, it was to get us safe home. We can't go back to look for her."

"But Mam ..."

"Weren't you listening? We came within an eyelash o' dying tonight, all of us. If Molly had anything to do with those fires, she might have had something in mind to save herself. Regardless, we can't save her." She turned to view the pinpricks of fires on the horizon growing smaller. "But I have no idea how she could have done *that*. The poor girl must be dead and drowned, God rest her soul."

The white ferret chittered at Granuaile as if he was scolding her. She looked at Eric in surprise, and then growled in response. "Oh, shut up, you. I'm going to miss her, too."

———

The ships rode out the storm and arrived at Rockfleet the following afternoon. The *Banshee* continued up to Burrishoole, where the harbor could accommodate unloading

King more easily. "He'll be glad to see his own stall again," Toby grinned.

"He'll be glad to get off the boat, more likely," Granuaile smiled. "Will ya be staying at Burrishoole for a bit, then?"

Toby thought for a moment. "No, I think I'll go back to Rockfleet with you first. Just to be certain."

Granuaile sighed. "Ya shouldn't be gettin' your hopes up. I lost friends, too, who didn't come back from Dublin prison with me. We all have our time."

"Yes," Toby whispered. *But this isn't Molly's time.*

Toby saw to King before they left, washing and grooming him before leaving him a generous helping of oats. They commandeered two ponies to ride back to Rockfleet. Granuaile was an excellent horsewoman herself, and they allowed themselves to gallop for a short way before settling down to a brisk walk.

"Am I to be puttin' up with that ferret now as well?" Granuaile teased.

"I doubt it. Eric is more independent than you think. I'll probably let him go if we don't find Molly."

"He helped Molly by biting that Joyce assassin. He's got a good heart, and I understand loyalty. Eric may stay as long as he wishes."

The ferret seemed to look at the queen and nod. He climbed up to Toby's shoulders and began chittering excitedly.

"Eric, what is it?" Toby exclaimed. "What do you see? We're almost at the castle — oh! Look, Mam!" He pointed ahead of them.

Granuaile followed her son's arm and drew an involuntary gasp.

Two figures stood on the road from Burrishoole to greet them. The taller was a stranger, a slim woman wearing a traveling cloak and carrying a bundle of scrolls.

The second was Molly O'Malley, dressed exactly as she had been the night Granuaile first saw her.

They spurred their steeds and galloped up to the pair. Granuaile swung out of her saddle as the pony came to a stop. She stared at the red-haired girl, then knelt and grabbed her shoulders. "How is this possible? Did one o' the galleys behind us pick ya up? Or did ya not go overboard at all, and were hiding somewhere when we looked for ya?"

"That's not important right now," Molly whispered. "Oh, Granuaile, I'm so glad you're safe!" She hugged the queen, burying her face in her neck.

The queen pushed Molly back, cradling her face in her calloused hands. "Ya called me Granuaile. You've not done that before."

"I know," Molly nodded. "'Bald Grace' seemed like a family name, that only those close to you should use. But I *do* love you. I love that little girl who cut off her hair and followed her heart to the sea. I was so afraid when I came here, and you showed me what it was like to be brave. My heart told me to protect you, because you have always protected everyone that depended on you. You're the one who taught me to never give up."

"That's right — never give up. Never." Granuaile crushed the girl to her bosom again. "I am Granuaile to you, and you are family to me."

"Molly?" Toby asked. "Who's this lady?"

"Oh, this is Lioc. She has something important to tell your mom. Toby, she — she's the one that Fionn sent for."

Toby turned as white as the ferret, who leaped from Toby's shoulder into Molly's arms. "Then — you're saying ..."

"Not yet. Go fetch a currach and meet us by the shore in a few minutes. Please?"

"What's going on? Who is Fionn?" Granuaile demanded.

"We need to go to your bedroom," Molly said. "Where this all began."

chapter twenty-four

Leavings

*G*ranuaile led the way up the winding stone staircase to the top of Rockfleet Castle. Molly and Lioc followed her into the flagstone-floored bedroom.

"All right, we're here. Now what is so interestin' about my bedroom?" The pirate planted her feet, hands on her hips.

"I don't know," Molly admitted. "Only that this is where I met you. Where I went back in time."

"Went back in time? What nonsense is this, Molly?"

Lioc stepped forward. "No nonsense, Grania," she said evenly. "Molly is a traveler from the future. She was drawn here to set things right, and she has done just that."

"I'll tell ya what I believe. I believe that I make my *own* history, and I don't need any storytellers making up fables." Granuaile spat on the polished stone floor.

"Do you believe that two children were able to outwit Nicholas Malby and free your people? Do you believe that Molly escaped from Malby's clutches and traveled across Connemara in one night — without a horse?" Lioc smiled. "Do you believe that Molly threw herself into the sea, and that the Barbary pirates' ships mysteriously burst into flame, leaving your fleet untouched? And that Molly then appeared here at Rockfleet, a day before the fleet returned?"

Granuaile chewed her lip slowly. "I can't deny what has happened. I can't explain it, but I refuse to give up responsibility for my own life!"

Lioc looked into Granuaile's eyes. "Do you believe that everything Molly has done, she did because she believes in you?"

The pirate queen looked at Molly, who shrank from the flashing eyes. "There are many who believe in me," Granuaile muttered.

"And more will, thanks to the brave heart of this O'Malley child." Lioc smiled warmly. "Granuaile, would you like to see some magic?"

Granuaile threw back her head and laughed, a rough, hearty sound that echoed down the stairs. "Aye, I'd like to see your parlour tricks!"

"It will not be for my parlour, but for yours. Molly, the medallion, please."

Molly slipped the gold chain over her head. Granuaile looked at the stone disk hung on it with interest.

"Where was the mark, Molly?" Lioc asked.

"Over here, on this wall." Molly walked to the bare wall just to the right of a plush sheepskin wall hanging. She looked around to gauge the angle to the fireplace. "Yes, this is where it was."

Lioc pressed the carved side of the medallion to the spot that Molly indicated. *"Tempus Aeternalis,"* the woman said in a clear, strong voice. The medallion began to glow blue, the light leeching into the surrounding stone as it, too, began to glow.

Lioc pulled the medallion away. Imprinted on the wall was the reverse image of the medallion's face, like a reflection seen in a mirror. The pattern lines glowed briefly like neon lights before fading back to the natural grey of the stone.

"What sorcery is this?" Granuaile demanded.

"This," Lioc breathed deeply, "Is what brings Molly back to you."

Granuaile stepped up to the new adornment and traced the indented edges with her finger. "Now *that's* a neat trick," she whispered.

"I wouldn't mention this to too many people," Lioc said cheerfully. "Magic isn't well thought of in many corners." Lioc handed the medallion back to Molly, who slipped it over her head.

"Wasn't planning on it," Granuaile grunted.

"This will be goodbye. Molly's actions have kept you alive and well for now."

"For how long?"

Lioc smiled darkly. "I cannot say more. Most people live only to forty in this age, and you are forty-nine already."

Granuaile chuckled. "But even the mighty Lioc would not bet against Grace the Gambler?"

Molly cleared her throat. "Granuaile, may I — may I hug you goodbye?"

The pirate queen looked down at Molly. "After all this, you are still a little girl. I'd hunt ya down and hug ya meself if ya didn't!" She knelt and swept the red-haired girl into a tight embrace.

Molly's last sight of the pirate queen was of the tall woman standing at her window staring out at Clew Bay, her eyes as molten as the blue waves stirred by the wind.

Molly decided to take advantage of the brief time they had alone before meeting Toby. "Lioc, or Clio, who are you, exactly?"

"My true name is Clio, but to all others I must remain known as Lioc, at least for now. I am a Muse, along with my eight sisters. Each of us has a special interest; art, music, dance. Mine is history."

"Oh, so that's why you're so interested in history. And you can even control time!"

"Only when needed." Clio smiled, tight-lipped. "Your presence in this time helped preserve the true history. Events would have been different if you hadn't come back."

"But now you're going to send me back home?"

"Yes, Molly. It's time for you to return home."

Toby was waiting for them at the shore, the little currach rocking in the surf.

"Where are we going?" he asked.

"The usual place," Molly smiled.

They rowed out beyond the first island and the white ferret changed into a leprechaun, red hair waving in the evening breeze. "Mercy, me, I don't know how much longer I could o' kept *that* up!" he exhaled.

"You make a splendid ferret, Eric," Molly beamed. "But you make a better friend."

Darkness covered them as they touched the sandy beach of Nefra's island. "I have a lamp so we can find the clearing," Toby said. "What are we doing out here again?"

"We're saying goodbye, Toby." Molly brushed back a tear. "To everyone."

They marched through the woods behind Toby's light. The clearing loomed silent and empty before them.

Molly flicked her heart-shaped locket open and held the shamrock in her palm.

"Out of time, out of myth,
I summon you now here forthwith.
Nefra, heir of the dragon race,
come now to this time and place."

The lamp flame flickered, and a huge black shape landed softly in the clearing. Two great yellow eyes glowed back at them.

"Thank you for coming, Nefra," Molly said.

"What, no danger? No imminent disaster to rescue you from? I was just getting used to the excitement of this summoning business." Nefra's voice laughed in the night.

"I'm going home. I wanted to say goodbye." Molly smiled. "First, Toby."

Toby would have been seen to blush if was brighter, but there was only the lamp to give light. Molly went to him and hugged him.

"Toby, you've been a grand friend to me! You taught me so much about riding, and boats — but mostly about being there for the people that need you. You went with me to Castle Hackett, and had that long ride across Connemara ... I couldn't be prouder to call you my friend!"

"Ah, Molly," he replied, "You've taught me so much about the fairy world, and dragons, and magic! And I can't breathe a word of it to anyone or they'll lock me up in the nearest dungeon!"

"At least you know that anything's possible." Molly grinned. "Remember that, always!"

"Don't I get a hug, now?" Eric smiled, his arms crossed over his apron.

"Oh, of course!" Molly swept him up and held him tightly. "I would have died if you hadn't bitten Richard Joyce. You protected Toby on that terrible ride, and helped so much to free Myles and little Seamus!"

"I wouldn't have been at all if it weren't for you, Molly," Eric said gently.

Molly set the little man down and turned to the dragon. "Nefra, I've been doing a lot of thinking about you. I'm going to meet you in the future. So you need to make sure you get there in one piece, and at the right time."

"I'll be careful," said the dragon.

"When you meet me, you can't say anything about how we met back in 1579 and helped save Granuaile from the English. You have to keep that secret from me."

Nefra nodded her great head. "I understand."

"And Nefra, dangerous times are coming. You need to hide away from men for another four hundred twenty-five years or so. Then go to the Burren. You'll find an underwater cave entrance off Galway Bay. And you'll have to start gathering gold from the leprechauns."

"Now wait just a minute!" Eric began.

"Oh, Eric, it's just so she can get to meet me! The leprechauns will have a problem, and Paddy will share it with me! The leprechauns will get all of their gold back!"

"Well, all right, then," Eric said dubiously.

"Now that I think about it, Nefra, you didn't seem to know what leprechauns were. So play dumb and say you thought they were just little men." Molly closed her eyes, trying to remember.

"Where will I hide until then?" Nefra asked.

"There's a big cave at the Cliffs of Moher, that would work for a while. You might try Scotland, I heard they have some big lakes there you could hide in. Oh, and the most important thing." Molly slipped the medallion from around her neck. "You'll need to understand English in case men get close to you. The more you know, the better you'll be able to hide. This medallion will let you understand English, and even talk to people in English if you need to. But try to stay hidden, okay?"

"That chain will never go around Nefra's neck," Eric observed.

"Gosh, I forgot about that. What can I — hey, I know!" Molly removed her pouch.

Laying it on the ground, she whispered 'water.' The material shimmered and moved under her touch as she stretched it into a long, thin strip of cloth about ten feet long. She held it up to Nefra's neck and the color shifted to a matching shade of black. "Ice," she said, and the transformation was complete.

"We'll tie the medallion on using this. I'll just keep the gold chain — Eric, don't look at me like that — and this will keep you safe."

"Thank you, Molly," Nefra murmured, and her voice echoed inside Molly's head.

"That's my Nefra," Molly smiled. She gave the dragon one last squeeze before walking back to Clio.

"I'm ready," she said. A tear slid down her freckled cheek.

"Yes, you are," Clio smiled. She handed Molly a scroll. The girl touched it and the paper disintegrated. Surprised, Molly looked up at the Muse, only to see her disintegrate as well. In fact, everything seemed to break into pieces and swirl around her. She felt dizzy, and then the pieces started slowing down, like a 1000-piece puzzle coming together. But it was not the same picture.

Molly found herself in the time-ravaged and deserted bedroom of Grania O'Malley. It was empty save for a small red-haired girl on the other side of the room, standing with her back to Molly. She appeared to be touching a necklace to a pattern on the wall.

Suddenly a 'bright blue light flashed and the girl vanished. Molly stumbled across the space and felt the wall. It was as smooth as the rest of it, with no sign of the pattern at all.

The blood pounded in Molly's ears. *Am I back? Am I really back?*

"Molly!" came her aunt's voice from down the stairwell. "Are ya goin' to spend the whole night in an empty bedroom? Come on, dear, before ya stir up a ghost!"

chapter twenty-five

Survivor

Molly looked at Croagh Patrick still filling the view from the car's rear window. "Is it much farther?"

"Louisburgh is just ahead," Sean O'Malley replied. "You've been crazy for Grace O'Malley ever since we visited Rockfleet!"

"It's *Granuaile*, Dad," Molly replied, batting her eyes. "Grace O'Malley is what the English called her."

"Fine then, Granuaile," he grinned. "I hope they have enough information at the visitor center to satisfy you!"

In the center of Louisburgh they pulled into the visitor center parking lot. "The building looks like an old church," Molly's mom said. "Look at the gothic windows with the pointed arches on top."

Molly's dad bought their admission tickets and they waited a few minutes for a tour. Fortunately attendance was light and a forty-ish woman in a royal blue pant suit soon greeted them. "Hello, I'm Erin Jennings. Looks like you folks get a private tour today!"

The Granuaile Visitor Centre didn't look big from the outside, but the inside held many fascinating things. Several dioramas painted on the walls seemed to spring right out at them, as real props matching the colors and textures made them look three dimensional. Molly liked the one with a life-size wax figure of Granuaile herself standing before a picture of a ship at sea, a cutlass hung at her side. It didn't look like the Granuaile she remembered, of course; this copy made the queen look about thirty years old. It captured her spirit, though, and Molly smiled, remembering the brave warrior she had left only yesterday.

"Erin, could you tell us about Granuaile after 1579?" Molly asked.

"Now *there's* a question we don't get every day!" Erin smiled. "Did you have anything specific in mind?"

"No, I'm just curious about what happened after she was released from Dublin prison and the English attacked Rockfleet that spring."

"Oh, my, that was an exciting time! In the latter part of 1579, the Earl of Desmond rose up in rebellion against the English. Richard-an-Iarainn, Granuaile's husband, raised an army and supported Desmond. Granuaile supported Richard as well. It didn't go well for them, however, as Governor Malby defeated Richard and drove him into hiding on the islands of Clew Bay by 1580."

"Oh, *Nicholas* Malby?" Molly groaned.

"My, you know your history, dear! Yes, Sir Nicholas Malby. Granuaile negotiated Richard's submission to Malby before the governor had to return to fighting Desmond."

"So that was it. Malby won out." Molly was about to cry.

"Oh, not at all! In the fall of 1580 the MacWilliam, who had supported the English, died. Richard pressed for his right to the MacWilliam title and Granuaile supported him. Together they raised a large force of fighting men. Malby ended up backing Richard-an-Iarainn to be the new MacWilliam, and he finally gained the title in 1581."

"So Malby didn't attack Granuaile?" Molly asked.

"No, he pretty much left her alone. Granuaile became wealthy as the new MacWilliam's wife. After that, other than fighting Desmond, I think Nicholas Malby was remembered mostly for building a new wing on the castle at Roscommon. Malby died in 1584."

"Sounds like your Granuaile had a pretty exciting life," Molly's dad grinned.

"That's just the beginning," Erin said. "According to some reports, Granuaile hosted gatherings of nobles as befit her new title of Lady Bourke, and she made quite an impression. Unfortunately, it didn't last long, as Richard died of natural causes in 1583."

"Oh no! What did she do?" Molly asked.

"She knew that she was not entitled to her second husband's property upon his death, so she gathered her possessions, a hundred followers, and returned to Rockfleet castle to claim it as her own."

"And became a pirate again?"

"And became a trader and a pirate again," Erin laughed. "Then the hard times started. In 1584 Richard Bingham was appointed governor of Connaught. He believed that the Irish could only be subdued by force. He particularly focused on Granuaile. To ensure that she would not cause problems, he captured and imprisoned her youngest son, Tibbot."

"He put Toby in prison? Oh, no!" Molly exclaimed.

"It was more of a house arrest, except for the possible threat of execution," Erin said. "Tibbot met and married his wife shortly before being imprisoned. He became good friends with her brother, which served him well in later life."

"That still doesn't sound good."

"Tibbot eventually escaped, but these were dark times. Bingham's brother, Captain John Bingham, attacked Granuaile's eldest son, Owen, at Bunowen. Owen was captured while trying to make peace with them, then bound and cruelly murdered."

"Owen? Murdered?" Molly gasped.

"Are you all right, dear? You're white as a sheet. Perhaps I shouldn't tell you all of these things ..."

"No! No, I want to know. I'm all right. Please go on." Molly took a deep breath.

"After Owen's murder Granuaile went on the attack against Bingham and the English, fighting alongside many of her former enemies who opposed Richard-an-Iarainn for the MacWilliamship. Bingham rounded up many of her relatives, and finally captured Granuaile herself. Bingham systematically killed most of his prisoners, and even had a gallows built for Granuaile to be hanged on."

"I can't believe that Granuaile would end up like that," Molly whispered.

"And you would be right. Granuaile's son-in-law, Richard the 'Devil's Hook,' who was married to her daughter Margaret, offered himself as hostage in her stead, and for some reason Granuaile was released. But Bingham continued to press, stripping Granuaile of her cattle and property, leaving her in poverty."

"Couldn't she support herself on the sea?" Molly cried.

"The English finally charted the Irish coastline, and were able to pursue and destroy any Irish raider. Granuaile was cut off from trading and piracy." Erin sighed.

"So they finally got a map," Molly said softly.

"Granuaile wasn't finished yet. When Murrough, her youngest son by Dónal, sided with the English, Granuaile sent an army and attacked him in a rage. She couldn't believe that he would do that after the murder of his brother."

"Wow. She attacked her own son." Molly shook her head.

Erin nodded. "Then came the worst times of all. Richard Bingham captured both Granuaile's half-brother and her son Tibbot and imprisoned them. He threatened to execute them both."

"No!" Molly gasped.

"Granuaile had given up trying to reason with Bingham, so she decided to go over his head. She sent letters back and forth to the English court, probably with the help of Tibbot before he was captured. Granuaile's contact in the court was Lord Burghley, Elizabeth's principal and most trusted advisor. Burghley sent her eighteen questions to answer before he would pass her requests on to the Queen. These questions are now part of the English state papers and tell us much of what we know of Granuaile today."

"So, did Queen Elizabeth help Granuaile?"

"After Bingham imprisoned Granuaile's half-brother and her son, Granuaile decided she could not wait any longer. In the summer of 1593 she set out in one of her last galleys, sailed around Ireland and England, and up the Thames River to London. There she requested a personal meeting with Queen Elizabeth."

"I *like* this lady," Aunt Shannon smiled.

"It was a meeting of two queens. They were nearly the same age, Granuaile being only three years older than Elizabeth. Both had become powerful leaders in a man's world, and so each had a measure of respect for the other."

"And *then* Queen Elizabeth helped Granuaile?" Molly pressed.

"First they had to have a talk. Elizabeth didn't speak Irish, and Granuaile didn't speak much English. It is believed that they held their discussions in Latin, which both queens spoke fluently. Granuaile made her case that she was twice-widowed, poor, and was being hurt by Richard Bingham in many ways. She carefully avoided talking about her piracy on the seas, or her support on the battlefield against the English from time to time. She asked Elizabeth to pardon her for any prior misdeeds against the Crown, restore her property, and free her half-brother and Tibbot."

"I've heard that people had their heads chopped off for less than that in Elizabeth's court," Molly's dad said.

"Quite true," Erin agreed. "However, Elizabeth was quite taken with this wild Irish queen. The guards searched Granuaile when she arrived and found a dagger. Granuaile said that it was strictly for her personal protection, and Elizabeth accepted her explanation readily.

"Another story tells that Granuaile had to sneeze, and one of the ladies of the court offered her a finely embroidered lace handkerchief. Granuaile used it, and then tossed it into a roaring fireplace. Elizabeth scolded her for treating such a fine gift that way, saying that she should have kept the handkerchief. Granuaile replied that the Irish were not savages, and that a used handkerchief was a filthy rag and ought to be destroyed. This seemed to amuse Elizabeth."

"Did it amuse Elizabeth enough to give Granuaile what she asked for?" Molly asked.

Erin smiled. "Yes, she gave Granuaile pretty much everything she asked for. There was to be no more fighting against the English or raiding their ships, but Granuaile was free to return to the sea in the name of the Queen. Elizabeth ordered Bingham to release his prisoners."

"I'll bet she was glad that was over," Molly grinned.

"Bingham still tried to do everything he could to hinder Granuaile without directly breaking Elizabeth's commands. He succeeded in keeping Granuaile's actions limited and her family in poverty for another two years. Finally, he was recalled to England and imprisoned himself."

"And then they got another English governor, I'll bet. Was the next one any better?" Molly grumbled.

"Actually, he was. Sir Conyers Clifford became well acquainted with Tibbot, and they became close allies."

"It seems strange that Tob — I mean, Tibbot — would side with the English after everything that had happened," Molly frowned.

Erin sighed. "It was because of the inter-clan rivalries that still existed. You see, Granuaile didn't regard the English as her enemies until they attacked her or got in her way. The other Gaelic lords often went against Granuaile and her clan, and when they did, Granuaile went to war with them, and sided with the English if they would help her. In 1595, the O'Donnell and the O'Neill, who held Ulster in the north of Ireland, decided to revive the MacWilliam title in Mayo. Unfortunately, they excluded Granuaile and her Bourke relations from the proceedings. That angered Granuaile and drove her to seek out English allies who were also trying to limit the power of Ulster."

"But weren't the O'Donnell and the O'Neill just doing what the Gaelic lords had always done, fighting among themselves?" Molly asked.

"Actually, this was the first time that anyone started thinking of themselves as Irish instead of just the member of a certain clan. Red Hugh O'Donnell led the attack, and his goal was to drive the English from Ireland and unite all of the clans as one nation. That's one of the problems the Irish had; the English *already* saw themselves as a nation. Late in the 16th century, the O'Donnells and the O'Neills finally realized this weakness and tried to convince the other remaining lords to join them, but it was too late. England had gained too strong a foothold."

"Did you say Red Hugh O'Donnell was leading the attack?" Molly asked in amazement.

"Yes," Erin said. "He became the O'Donnell after his father, and was one of the strongest forces for Irish unity against the English."

I can believe that, Molly thought. "What happened to Tibbot?"

"Tibbot was quite resourceful, like his mother. With the help of the English, he started to assemble much of the land in County Mayo under his control. In 1597 he actually gave the title of the MacWilliamship to a relative of his. But the title didn't matter any more, as Tibbot already owned all of the land that used to go with the office. By giving the title to someone else, he showed that he was *greater* than the MacWilliam."

Way to go, Toby! "Is that the end of the story, then?" Molly asked.

"Almost. By 1601 the O'Donnells and the O'Neills were desperate. They tried for one last victory by convincing the Spanish to help them by invading Ireland and merging their forces. The Spanish, however, landed at Kinsale in the south of Ireland, clear across the island from where the Ulster forces were."

"Brilliant!" Molly snorted. "No wonder they had problems."

"O'Donnell and O'Neill marched across Ireland to Kinsale to besiege the forces of the English commander, Lord Mountjoy, who was in turn besieging the Spanish. Tibbot raised a force of 300 men and in December marched to Kinsale himself. For three months neither the O'Donnell nor Mountjoy knew which side Tibbot would take in the final battle."

"Well?" Molly demanded breathlessly.

Erin grinned. "He threw his forces in with the English and defeated the Gaelic and Spanish forces. The Battle of Kinsale was the final event that ended Gaelic rule in Ireland and sealed England's victory. Tibbot was able to use his alliance with the English to hold on to his land and possessions in County Mayo. Eventually he became the first Viscount of Mayo, a prestigious title of nobility and power."

Molly sighed. "And what about Granuaile?"

"We don't know for sure, but she probably died in 1603 at Rockfleet. Queen Elizabeth died the same year. They shared amazing lives that changed two nations. Granuaile lived to see the end of the Gaelic culture that she grew up in. But she survived, as did her children, to adapt to the new world order."

"An amazing woman," Molly's mom whispered.

"Totally," Molly agreed.

chapteʀ twenty-six

Adventure's End

the sky was a brilliant cobalt blue for a change, dotted with puffy clouds that floated slowly over the Aran Islands on their way to Connemara. Molly watched from her seat reclining against the north wall of the ringfort.

"Paddy," she yawned, handing him another apple, "Do you think I could have imagined it all?"

"Some imagination, I'd say," he chuckled. "Ye gave the medallion to Nefra, didn't ye? How else would she have been able to give it to you last summer?"

"Yes, I suppose that's true." The red-haired girl gazed across the bay at Galway. "I flew on a dragon, right along there, all the way from Galway City to Bunowen." She swept her arm from right to left as she pointed. "Now all I have left are memories, and I can only share them with a few special people."

"Molly, what's gotten into ye? Ye still have the enchanted bracelet, and the fine boots I made ye, and the shamrock that ye used to make the wishes and summon Nefra! There's nuttin' wrong with memories, either! To tell the truth, I have many fond memories of our adventures together!"

Molly shot the leprechaun a dubious look. "To tell the truth? Did you cast a *firinne* spell when I wasn't looking?" She sighed. "I know I have no reason to complain, but the medallion meant so much to me, and the magic cloth was a special gift from Queen Meb. I'm just going to miss them, that's all."

Paddy bit into his apple and chewed for a few seconds. "At least Granuaile and Toby came out all right, from what they told ye at that Visitor Centre. Ye set history right, Molly, and that's somethin' to be proud of."

"That's not all. I learned how to ride a horse, and row a boat, and be an actress, and be ever-so-conniving. I hid things from people who were dear to me."

"And from what ye've told me, ye had to do those things to protect them. Ye were far braver than any twelve-year-old I've seen. Didn't ye mention that Finvarra said the same thing?"

"Oh, yes, it *was* wonderful seeing Fionn again." Molly closed her eyes to remember. "He's really cute all grown up, too."

"Forget it, me dear, he's been married for hundreds o' years now, and is quite settled as the King o' the Fairies. Ye'll find a young man o' your own some day. Ye'll be much better off if ye don't pick one from the pages o' history!"

"If you're talking about Toby, we were only friends. Really close friends, but that's all. And Fionn has only kissed me on my forehead and my hand." She raised one hand to her cheek and lifted her other hand dramatically into the air. "Just before he gave me the weather report! Oh, man, what a kiss *that* was!"

She broke into convulsive giggles, which Paddy found to be contagious. Finally they wiped the tears from their eyes and looked at each other.

"So tell me, Molly, what was Granuaile really like?"

She looked across the bay, following the path of a gull with her eyes. "She was the most incredibly persistent person I have ever met. Granuaile didn't let anything stop her if she wanted something. She rebuilt the O'Flaherty trading fleet, became a pirate to survive — although I think she really *enjoyed* being a pirate, too — and became a leader in a world that didn't make it easy for a woman to accomplish anything. When I think of the hardships she went through, poor Owen being murdered, Granuaile being imprisoned twice, having Toby locked up and scheduled for execution — she is made of sterner stuff than I am."

"Don't ye go sellin' yourself short now, Molly O'Malley!" Paddy scolded. "Ye risked your own neck for her. I didn't hear of anyone else pushin' ye off that ship in the middle o' the Atlantic!"

"Okay, so we're both persistent. And I have to say that we both have had interesting lives. Although I think my life is going to be a lot less interesting from now on. I'm running out of magic talismans."

Paddy sighed. "It's right ye are, Molly. No one is goin' to think twice about a colleen whose best friend is a leprechaun."

"No one is going to think at all because they'll never know." Molly smiled. "Oh, well. Like you said, I have my memories. And I'll be back again next summer. Unless you have another magic coin I can borrow ...?"

"No, I don't think so. Security at the Royal Treasury seems to have been beefed up since the old days. King Finvarra knows somethin' about the ways o' *this* wayward leprechaun." He grinned and finished his apple. "I'm becomin' a bit more patient in me old age."

"Old age, my foot! You just turned 400!" Molly stood up. "I need to be getting back. We're leaving in the morning. Oh, and Paddy, if you happen to run into an elderly leprechaun with red hair who goes by the name of Eric O'Malley ... ?"

"I'll be sure to give him your best," Paddy smiled. "Perhaps he was just waitin' for ye to get back before he reintroduces himself."

"Thanks. Well, it was grand to see you again, Paddy!" She knelt and hugged the little man gently.

"Molly? There's one thing I've been meanin' to ask ye. No one knows what Granuaile really looked like. But ye've seen her! What *did* the pirate queen look like?"

"Ooh, that really hard to say. She was tall, strong, when I saw her she had salt-and-pepper hair, and her skin was weathered from being near the ocean. I'm sorry. I've never been good about describing people. That's about all I can tell you."

"Well, for example, what color eyes did she have?"

Molly smiled. "Oh, that's an easy one. Her eyes were always the color of the sea."

epilogue

Coming Home

Rockfleet Castle, 1603

he sisters had come from the Cisterian Abbey on Clare Island to pray for the soul of Granuaile.

Not that I've visited there often, Granuaile thought. *Yet my father and I have sponsored the order there and at Murrisk for decades. Let them pray, if it will make them feel better. I have no regrets.*

The pirate queen was failing at last. Seventy-three years of toil on land and sea had taken its toll, not to mention numerous hardships at the hands of English and Irish lords alike. Yet she had survived. She was still breathing, free in her own beloved Rockfleet, the symbol of her independence.

It was she who proposed marriage to Richard-an-Iarainn, and she who had leaned from these very castle ramparts to dismiss him from their "trial" marriage a year later. *Ah, Richard, ya never did quite know what to do with me, did ya my love? But ya gave me the freedom I needed to be myself. We were a grand team, weren't we, my MacWilliam?* Granuaile's eyes fluttered and the intensity of the chants around her intensified.

No, not yet. Granuaile forced her mind to clarity again. *I've lived a full life, been bolder than any man I led into battle. I cheated the devil many a time, and lived to see my children come of age. Owen ...* A tear trickled down her weathered cheek. *But Toby, he'll do well.*

He's learned to walk the tightrope between friend and foe, to recover from loss, to prosper, to survive. Already he is the most powerful Gael in Mayo.

Intermixed with the prayers of the sisters she could hear the waves of Clew Bay spraying against Rockfleet's foundations. *High tide again. The sea has given me so much, has given me everything ...*

How had she survived so long, overcome so much in one lifetime? *My will, my spirit, my destiny,* she thought ... *but not mine alone.*

With effort she turned her head to the wall. It was still there, after all these years. The imprint in the stone of a circle, a serpent swallowing itself surrounded by a triangle and encircling a mystic eye. It was a stark reminder of another light in a dark day, another soul refusing to yield to defeat. *Molly.* The strange girl from another time who risked everything for her, and won.

Now the death rattle rose in her throat. But Granuaile was at peace. *I know that there is still one who will carry the O'Malley spirit with them into the future. I'm glad to have known ya, Molly O'Malley.*

Granuaile passed from life with a smile on her cracked lips.

Molly dragged her suitcase up onto the bed and flopped down to rest for a minute. "Wow, I never thought that a cheeseburger and a vanilla shake could taste so wonderful. But then, I never spent four months in the 16th century before, either!"

She sighed and began unpacking. Jeans and slacks in the bottom drawer, shirts in the middle drawer, socks in the top ...

She paused, frowning as something blocked her socks from sliding easily to the back. She opened the drawer all the way and fished around for the cause. "What in the world ..."

Molly drew out a bundle of folded cloth, worn and blackened. It had the look of a fine weave to it, if you looked closely. She stared at it for a moment, then her eyes widened in recognition.

The girl gently unfolded the fabric on her plush red comforter. The cloth was about ten feet long when unrolled, and a few inches wide.

Scarcely daring to breathe, Molly touched the ancient cloth and murmured *"Water."*

The cloth shimmered and softened, mimicking the color and texture of the comforter. Molly pushed the length into a pile and spread it out again like soft clay, where it responded eagerly to her touch.

"Nefra's band that held the medallion. My gift from the Fairy Queen," she whispered. "It was here all the time."

Molly smiled. The shape of the magic cloth, like her future, was in her hands.

author's note

Everyone's intrigued by a pirate.

From Long John Silver in the classic *Treasure Island*, to the infamous and real life Edward Teach (Blackbeard), to the modern Captain Jack Sparrow in *Pirates of the Caribbean*, children and adults alike are drawn to these symbols of independence despite their other unsavory qualities.

Imagine my delight in discovering Grace O'Malley, pirate queen of the western Irish seas who carved her place in history during the 16th century. Known as Granuaile to the Irish, she refused to be bound to the traditional place of the woman as housekeeper in her culture. Instead she took on roles that were difficult enough for men: seafaring, politics, and piracy.

Molly O'Malley and the Pirate Queen blends the reality of the legendary Granuaile and her family with the fantasy and magic that Ireland is blessed with. Molly learns much about courage, sacrifice, and the will to never give up in the face of difficulty.

These are lessons we can all use. Even if you don't happen to be a pirate.

Duane Porter

glossary

Term	Definition
Anamith	The Soul Eater. Fatal to fairies, very nasty to humans.
bodhrán	A thin, circular drum much like a tambourine but without the bells around the edge. It is played by striking it with a stick.
Bruionn	A bard in the O'Donnell's court.
Bunowen	A castle, port and surrounding lands in the far west of Connemara. It was the principal ruling location for the O'Flaherty clan. Granuaile's eldest son Owen O'Flaherty lived there after his father Dónal died.
Burren	A unique part of western Ireland with much limestone, many caves, and a wide variety of plants and flowers that grow there.
cathair	A stone ringfort. Molly discovered a ringfort in the Burren.
colleen	Irish name for girl.
Connaught	The central west region of Ireland, one of the four major provinces. It is made up of the counties of Galway, Mayo, Roscommon, Sligo and Leitrim.
Connemara	The southwest region of Galway, known for its rugged mountains and long seacoast bordering Galway Bay and the Atlantic Ocean.
Croagh	Irish for mountain. Croagh Patrick is therefore "St. Patrick's mountain."
Eire	The gaelic, or Irish name for Ireland.

Term	Definition
Fannléas	The Irish name for Glimmer, the fairy realm where ideas can become real.
Fionn / Finvarra	Queen Meb's son, who is replaced by a changeling. His name means "fair." He grows up to become the next King of the Fairies after Molly helps him.
Gaelic	The old language of Ireland. Gaelic, or Irish, is now the official language of the country again, with English being a second official language.
Galway	The county bordering the north shore of Galway Bay, taking in Connemara and Galway City.
Grania, Granuaile, Grace O'Malley, Grainne Mhaol (bald Grace)	Famous daughter of a Gaelic chieftain, Granuaile led the O'Malleys and a large number of the O'Flaherty clan to build a shipping empire. She engaged in piracy when needed. Most of what we know about her comes from accounts in English state papers of the time. Grania does hold a place in Irish legends and songs.
Kildownet	A Norman style tower castle on the southeast coast of Achill Island, part of Granuaile's network of fortifications ringing Clew Bay. It is informally called "Grace O'Malley's Castle."
Rockfleet	Granuaile's principal and most beloved castle. She acquired it by marrying Richard-an-Iarainn and "divorcing" him a year later. They remained close.

Term	Definition
la poupe	A French term meaning the stern, or the back of a ship, generally raised above the level of the main deck. It is from this term that we get the name "poop deck."
Labhras	A king in an Irish folk tale who had his hair cut only once every three years, then executed his barber to protect his secret — that the king had horses' ears.
Lioc / Clio	One of the nine muses. Clio's specialty is history, while her sisters inspire art, music, astronomy, and dance. She often travels using the anagram name of Lioc.
Lough Corrib	Lake Corrib, a large lake in County Galway that separates the eastern region from Connemara to the west.
Lough Mask	Lake Mask, a smaller lake to the north of Lough Corrib.
Mayo	A northwestern county in Connaught. It is traditionally home to the O'Malley clan in the area of Clew Bay.
Richard-an-Iarainn (Granuaile's second husband)	"Iron Richard," nicknamed either for an ancient iron breastplate he liked to wear, or for the ironworks he owned at Burrishoole. Second husband to Granuaile. Their son is Tibbot-ne-Long.
Tibbot-ne-Long (Granuaile's youngest son)	"Toby of the Ships," so named because he was born at sea on his mother's ship. Toby survived the English invasion to become the first Viscount of Mayo.

Term	Definition
the MacWilliam	A Gaelic title traditionally held by the Bourkes in County Mayo. Granuaile's second husband, Richard-an-Iarainn became the MacWilliam in 1581.
the O'Donnell	A Gaelic title similar to the MacWilliam which governed the area of Tyrconnell in modern County Donegal.
Roscommon	A county east of Mayo and Galway. Nicholas Malby made Roscommon Castle there his principal estate.
Sir Nicholas Malby	Appointed Governor and President of Connaught by Queen Elizabeth, he worked to bring the rebellious Irish under the control of England in the late 16th century.
tanaiste	The second in line (literally *understudy*) to a major Gaelic title. Granuaile's first husband Dónal was tanaiste for the O'Flaherty but was killed before obtaining it. Her second husband Richard Bourke was tanaiste for the MacWilliam and he did eventually gain the title.
Tiarnach	The castle where the Fairy King and his court live. The name means "Lord."

Available from amazon.com
in print or Kindle format.

Duane Porter
Buried Treasure Publishing
2813 NW Westbrooke Circle
Blue Springs, MO 64015
(816) 210-4314

Books by Duane Porter:

Molly O'Malley and the Leprechaun

Molly O'Malley: Rise of the Changeling

Molly O'Malley and the Pirate Queen

Charlie and the Chess Set

The Seirawan Factor

The Best Ride

Made in the USA
San Bernardino, CA
08 April 2014